Daniel Taylor

Carol Maginn

Copyright © 2015 by Carol Maginn
Photography: vali_111
Design: Soqoqo Design
Editor: Sue Barnard

No part of this book may be used or reproduced in any manner whatsoever without written permission of the author or Crooked Cat Books except for brief quotations used for promotion or in reviews. This is a work of fiction. Names, characters, and incidents are used fictitiously.

First Green Line Edition, Crooked Cat, 2015

Discover us online:
www.crookedcatbooks.com

Join us on facebook:
www.facebook.com/crookedcat

Tweet a photo of yourself holding
this book to **@crookedcatbooks**
and something nice will happen.

*To my lovely mum,
Win*

Firstly, thanks:

With thanks to my friends in Rome, to Crooked Cat, and to my editor Sue Barnard, and my friends who patiently read this in draft, with massive thanks.

About the Author

Carol Maginn was born in Liverpool, and has lived in Manchester, Sheffield, Kokopo, Rome and Edinburgh. She's currently writing, teaching English as a second language, and learning to dance salsa.

Chapter One

The Leonardo Express pulled into Rome in the gathering sunset. Daniel could see the woman standing close to the wall; a straight, slim figure, her hair riffling slightly in the breeze, a briefcase set down neatly at her feet. Had she not received his text? He sent the message again. He was grateful, of course, but there was no need for them to meet. No need, either, for the hotel which had been booked – he would make his own arrangements. If he needed anything, he'd let her know. Polite but clear, he felt. He left the train and allowed himself to be absorbed by the crowds that eddied through the station and surged through the main doors.

As he walked through the city, the golden sunset faded. His route followed a tram line, past the long covered market and the Chinese shops, through one of the gateways in the ancient city wall, and on into the neighbourhood of San Giovanni. He had an idea of where he would stay, and finally arrived at a tall, narrow albergo where there was a single room vacant on the 7th floor. His clothes took up very little space in the capacious set of drawers. Having unpacked, he leaned out of the window and slowly inhaled the night air. The sounds of traffic and conversation rose from the busy street below him, and he found that he was on eye level with the statues of Christ and his Apostles that gazed out from the roof of the illuminated Basilica San Giovanni Laterno.

A single vodka at a local bar would be a good end to the day – a quiet toast to the fact that he'd arrived. He glimpsed himself in the wardrobe mirror as he headed for the door; a tall, thin man whose hair was just beginning to recede at the temples, and whose default expression, which was stern, belied the fact that he was quite pleased to have got this far without interference from his client.

Chapter Two

"Of course it isn't convenient, Dan."

Jack Drummond, MP, stared at his constituency caseworker as if he had, before his very eyes, become a difficult six-year-old. It was a look he often used on parliamentary colleagues. "How do you think we're going to manage here?"

Dan's eyebrows rose.

"Exactly," Jack snapped. "I'm sorry, Dan, but it's just not on. You want to take leave, that's fine, but you book it well in advance and you okay it with me. You don't just... announce that you're going on holiday. You're not in the public sector now, you know."

Well, technically he was, but he didn't make a point of it. He repeated what he'd already said several times – brother, wedding, USA.

Jack shook his head. "And then you're tagging on two weeks – two weeks – in Rome. Come on, Dan. Either you want this job or you don't."

Dan didn't care. He was going. He had booked flights and blocked out his diary. Two weeks was no big deal. He could have been off with 'flu. Plus they had the intern, Lucy. She was the daughter of friends of Jack's, a cool blonde who at the age of twenty-one already had Parliamentary ambitions. Sometimes, when Dan looked into her uncomprehending blue eyes, he felt that he saw the next generation of Conservative MPs, and he felt overwhelmed with weariness.

Now, however, he gave her a list of potential emergency situations in which she was to call the Law Centre, the names of constituents he was dealing with who might ring, phone numbers and organisations to refer people to, and local solicitors who could be contacted.

She nodded, brushing her fringe from her deep blue eyes, and said, "Don't worry, Dan. You have a lovely time."

This was actually quite nice of her, so he said, "Thanks, Lucy," in a gruff kind of way, and prepared for his trip.

He'd arrived in Rome in the midst of a long, hazy sunset. His taxi swung him through the city, its pink skies streaked with underlit cloud, and deposited him outside his huge hotel. At reception, an immaculately polite young man handed him the key to the penthouse suite. "Enjoy your stay with us, Mr Taylor."

Dan said, "I think there's been a mistake here. I didn't book a suite…"

But the young man, having glanced at the computer screen, said, "No mistake, Mr Taylor. Will you take dinner with us tonight?"

He decided that he would. When in Rome… The room situation could be sorted out tomorrow. He could afford one night of luxury. After a long shower, he changed and sipped a Campari soda in the roof-top bar, watching as night fell and the lights of Rome shone beneath him. Then a leisurely meal of cannelloni and salad in the grand dining room. And when he finally laid his head on the down pillows, and stretched out in the king-size circular bed, he had barely time to register how completely and utterly comfortable he was before he fell asleep.

Chapter Three

Daniel Taylor was one of the first customers at the nearby bar when it opened the next morning. It was a cool, bright day. At the counter, people congregated two or more deep, still wrapped up for winter, sipping coffee and munching cornetti, mostly in sombre morning silence. As they left, each space was filled as those behind them placed their receipts on the counter, with the sound of the great hissing coffee machine forming a constant background. Daniel sat outside for some time, with a cappuccino and the local paper, and formulated his day's plan. The busy morning grew busier. Scooters navigated in and out of the traffic, horns sounded, and the flower-seller opposite uncovered his display. School children and office workers wove their way along the pavement. Soon the first tourists would be arriving to visit the Basilica, the parish church of Rome... Time to move. He had just signalled for his bill when a red-haired woman, dressed in a white shirt and business suit, crossed the road to the bar, unhurriedly and unmistakeably heading for him. She reached his table and seated herself opposite to him.

"Really, Mr Taylor," she said, putting her briefcase down beside her, "anyone would think you were trying to avoid me." Her grey eyes met his enquiringly, and he smiled and said, "I take it you're Sophia."

She smiled in return, and inclined her head.

"I'm just avoiding everybody," he said. "It's nothing personal."

"Well, you know what our client is like," Sophia said. "He wants you to have support."

He wants me watched because he's a mistrustful thug, is what Daniel thought, but didn't say.

"And, of course, this is my city," Sophia added. As if to

prove her point, a busy waiter abruptly changed course to come over and take her order.

Daniel said, "I appreciate the offer of help, Sophia. As I said in my text. But I've known Rome a long time."

"Your Italian isn't bad," she replied, sounding kind. "But our client thinks you may need backup. That's why I've been retained."

Daniel said, "Well, if I need backup, I'll be happy to call you." But he wasn't going to need it. Working with the mad Russian had been like this from the beginning. Plenty of unwanted help.

"It's been good to meet you," he said briskly, standing up and extending his hand. She took it.

"You too, finally," she said. "We'll stay in touch," she added, with her cool smile.

Daniel strode away, shaking his head. Private investigators, for reasons he had never understood, always thought they knew everything. Whereas he... he had a lot to do, and just two weeks in which to do it.

His client, and Sophia's, was the Russian, who had the calculating, twinkly eyes of the classic psychopath. In Daniel's opinion. He was in his forties, a bulky man in a handmade Italian suit. They had met in Budapest. The Russian hadn't risen when Daniel entered the restaurant, but had gestured him to a seat beside him, and grasped his hand. Then he had moved aside the remains of a meal of pork and peppers.

"So – the famous Daniel Taylor," he'd said, turning his whole body the better to scrutinise him. "I'm pleased to meet you at last. You're not so easy to get hold of."

Daniel had smiled briefly and shrugged, and waited for the Russian to get down to business. He'd noted the two silent men who sat at the table behind them, indifferently looking over the menu.

"Your reputation is good," the Russian said. "Very good. In fact, I probably should have commissioned you first, instead of the other one."

Daniel poured a glass of water and taken a sip.

"You think you can do this?" the Russian asked, and he'd nodded.

"Yes, I think I probably can."

"Good," the Russian said. "You know, I've heard some people say that you're arrogant, but then, some people say that I'm arrogant as well." He raised his eyebrows, and then his arms, helplessly, to express just how ridiculous this was. "I simply know my own mind, which is not a crime, and I can see that you know yours. That's good, Daniel."

He got to his feet, and the two men behind him did the same.

"And now you come with me," the Russian said cheerfully. "My jet is at the airport. Let me show you my collection. Then we'll understand each other."

And so they had flown to St. Petersburg.

Of course he'd been impressed. Not only with the house itself, an early eighteenth-century palace surrounded by parkland and security, but with what it contained.

"Naturally we learned a little about the Roman emperors in school," his host said, as they paced an echoing hall along a row of unquestionably authentic Roman busts, mounted on plinths. "Julius Caesar, Nero, all the usual. All the battles. But we didn't learn enough about what the Romans actually achieved, Mr Taylor. How they ran empires, century after century. Vast, vast administrative undertakings. Organised, disciplined, admirable."

He paused before one of the busts. "And here he is."

They both looked at the sightless face of Diocletian, third-century Roman Emperor and reformer. His eternal expression was one of exasperation. He'd been a bold ruler, and had succeeded in pulling the Roman Empire back from dissolution. It was interesting that he was admired by a twenty-first-century Russian oligarch. The Russian had a slightly ramshackle, though expensive, collection of the artefacts of various emperors – ceremonial daggers, short cloaks, brooches and fibulas, and rings. He looked at Daniel.

"Now you understand why I want the ring," he said. "I'm a serious collector."

Daniel nodded, but the Russian raised a finger to forestall anything he might be about to say.

"Most of what you hear about me is nonsense," he said. "As I'm sure you realise. I'm a cultivated and educated man. Self-educated. I've succeeded through hard work and good luck and good friends, and I make sure I thank my friends. My enemies…" He shrugged. "Who doesn't have enemies? We all do. You think Diocletian didn't have enemies? My God. But there he is…" He turned again towards the bust. "He was the only Roman emperor who retired, did you know that? He lived to grow cabbages."

The hall was cold, and one of the two uniformed men who guarded the door discreetly shifted from one foot to the other. The alarm system quietly blinked in each corner of the room.

"Of course I understand that this isn't just any ring," the Russian said. "That's why I've hired you. And you understand that I want it quickly, and without… fuss." They began to walk back towards the doorway, their footsteps sounding on the marble floor. "The previous expert, as you know, was an academic. He wrote a lot, but came up with nothing. In the end I had to let him go. I'll give you his report and his research notes." He glanced at Daniel. "It's possible that he wasn't a very good expert," he said conversationally. "Or it's possible that I wasn't paying him enough. What do you think, Mr Taylor?"

Daniel shrugged.

"Doctor Loggi?" he said. "I've heard of him. He's quite well known in his field."

"That's what I thought," the Russian said. "So perhaps the problem was money."

"Or perhaps the ring just isn't findable," Daniel said.

There was a silence. Then, casually, "Tell me, what is your hunch, Mr Taylor?"

"I'm afraid I don't have hunches."

The Russian smiled, unexpectedly pleased by this.

"I have confidence in you," he said, putting a heavy arm round Daniel's shoulders. "I think you'll do very well." He nodded, to emphasise his approval. "And you understand what a timetable means." He lowered his voice confidentially. "I'm getting married," he explained.

This was a surprise to Daniel. The Russian had just gone through a long and acrimonious divorce which his wife had brought in London, and which had been widely reported in the British media due to the vast sums involved. The most fiercely contested part of the settlement had been a Manhattan apartment, which he had been obliged to give up.

"My fiancée is a beautiful, very loving girl," he said. "Nothing like that bitch I was married to. When we exchange rings, she wishes to give me the ring of Diocletian as my wedding ring." He beamed, just a little complacently. "You know what women are like." He let his arm drop from Daniel's shoulders. "It is right that I have this ring," he said. "If people say that I'm doing this just to belittle a competitor... Well, you know the truth now." He gestured behind him, towards the darkening hall.

Daniel nodded.

"And you're happy to be paid on results," the Russian said. "Excellent. An admirable attitude."

And so the deal was done.

On the flight back to London, he glanced at the previous expert's report. Dr Francesco Loggi was a rising star at the University of South Milan, a respected young historian who had presented a TV series on the Roman Emperors and produced a coffee-table book to accompany the programmes. The report was dense, and Daniel skimmed through it. Outside the aircraft, the sky was a searing blue above a bed of thick cloud. He viewed sketches of the ring in question, and some old black and white photographs. Roman men, even emperors, generally wore no jewellery apart from their signet rings. They were simple, used to seal documents, and bore a design unique to their owner. Diocletian, despite a taste for jewelled gowns, had been no exception. His signet ring had been made of sardonyx, a banded red and white stone, and had borne the profile of a lion's head. However, what was fact, and what was legend, had very quickly merged.

Diocletian, Daniel read, had been the last of the Roman emperors to take a stand against Christianity and enforce the worship of the traditional Roman gods. He had made bold changes to the Empire's coinage, taxation, and law, and the elimination of religious minorities like Christians was simply a part of his campaign. It couldn't have helped that the Christian church in Nicodemia, where Diocletian was based, had been built on a hill overlooking his imperial palace.

Loggi had gone into considerable detail: Diocletian's first edict in AD303 had been that all churches and Christian documents should be destroyed, but without bloodshed – though this hadn't prevented Christians from being burnt alive as their churches burned. The second edict had ordered the imprisonment of all clergy. This had led to a logistical problem, as there wasn't enough prison space, and criminals had had to be released to fit all the clergy in. The third edict was an amnesty, providing that the clergy would be freed if they made sacrifices to the Roman gods. Some did, some refused; some, according to contemporary accounts, were told they had sacrificed whether they had or not, and were released anyway. The fourth edict, in AD304, commanded the whole population, on pain of death, to gather in public places and make collective sacrifices. This edict extended to Diocletian's own wife and daughter, who it seems were Christian.

Loggi had also included in his appendices a reproduction of Il Sodoma's The Martyrdom of St Sebastian. There he was, a naked and beautiful youth, his eyes turned towards Heaven, his white skin punctured by the arrows which had been fired at him, a figure of tranquil submission to the will of God. This was the Renaissance view of Sebastian, whereas in fact the real Sebastian had been a middle-aged soldier. Diocletian, ignorant of Sebastian's Christianity, had appointed him a captain of the Praetorian Guard. When he found out, the Emperor accused Sebastian of betrayal, and ordered him to be taken to a field and shot with arrows.

The point about this martyrdom was that Sebastian had managed to survive it. He had been found alive and nursed by a Christian widow, Irene of Rome. He had lived to stand on a step and harangue Diocletian as he passed by on a litter. The irritated Emperor now ordered him to be clubbed to death and his body thrown into the drainage system. And this was done.

However, there was also a legend, of unclear origin, that Diocletian had been so incensed by Sebastian that he had ordered his litter to be stopped. He had confronted him, throwing down his ring and ordering Sebastian to pick it up as a gesture of submission to the Roman state. Sebastian had refused, and a guard had struck him, so that drops of his blood had fallen onto Diocletian's ring. None of this would have been of any significance had Sebastian not turned out to be a most important saint, the third saint of Rome, and protector of plague victims and soldiers. And the ring of Diocletian had become known as Sebastian's ring, blessed by the martyr's blood with miraculous powers of healing.

This was the ring he was looking for. The difference between Daniel Taylor and Francesco Loggi was that searches such as this were exactly what Daniel specialised in. He could absorb information, retain it while he needed it, and then let it go again. His drive was not for knowledge, but for the solving of puzzles. It was what he did. It was, in fact, all he did.

"You know, of course, that there are other parties who are interested," the Russian had said confidentially, as his limousine whisked Daniel silently back to the airport. "Italians – you know what they're like – they think they have some sort of God-given right to things." He shook his head, mystified. "Ridiculous. But even so, we will need to be careful, Daniel." He handed him a mobile phone. "Use this, and only this. It's completely secure. We need to be quiet. Not too obvious." He smiled his wide, cunning smile and embraced Daniel as they stood in the departure lounge. "I'll be in touch," he said.

Chapter Four

"You don't like the suite?"

"Yes, I like it," Dan said. "But it isn't what I booked."

The receptionist regarded him. "It isn't...?"

"It isn't what I booked. I booked a room. Just a room."

He watched the receptionist checking on the computer screen.

"No, Mr Taylor. I have your booking here. You're here for two weeks, right?"

"Yes, that's right."

"Then the suite is yours."

"But I can't afford a suite. I just want a room."

Again, a quick flick over the keyboard.

"Payment has been made in advance, Mr Taylor. The suite is yours for fourteen nights."

This was the end of the matter as far as the receptionist was concerned. He turned to a couple waiting to check out, and Dan shuffled to one side. There was clearly a mistake. Clearly. He'd need to sort it out. But meanwhile, he had to get moving, and find his way to the Museum – his History of Italian Art course was starting in half an hour's time. He'd talk to the hotel people again tonight.

Map in hand, he stepped out into the busy Rome morning. He was here. He walked purposefully, aware that he looked very tourist-like in his new chinos and trainers. He had brought a notebook and a pen. This whole trip was an extravagance, but somehow he had come to a point where he didn't care any more. He was approaching forty years of age. He had never been to Italy. He'd never seen any of the works of the Italian masters. Whereas now he was going to see everything that the magnificent city had to offer.

He inhaled the air of Rome, smelt coffee, smelt (he

thought) croissants, or possibly pizza, and felt a very long way from home in a very good way. He would buy postcards. He would take pictures with his new camera, bought specially for this trip, and post them on Facebook. He would explore the city, eat Italian food, and let the debt, housing, and immigration problems of Jack's constituents be fielded by Lucy. Not that she... He stopped the thought in its tracks. He wasn't going to think about work. He was only here for two weeks, and he needed to make the most of it.

Titian. Rafael. Leonardo. Caravaggio. The sheer... splendour. Dan let the prospect of it all wash over him like fizzy water. He could feel the knot between his shoulder blades beginning to loosen. This was what he had come for – to admire beauty, and swagger, and talent. To forget about his brother, his job, and, basically, his life. To soak in art and become, once again, a student. Someone optimistic.

He would see if he could go and listen to an opera. He would visit the Vatican Museums... And then he was there, at the huge Palazzo Braschi, which housed the Museo. He showed his letter, was given a visitor pass, and was led along corridors and up echoing staircases until he came to the room where his first class was about to commence.

The lecture room had a wide table at its centre, and Dan took his place, nodding hellos to the other students. Eva, who was to be their tutor, was a sombre, elegant, middle-aged woman who wore small emerald ear-rings and spoke perfect English.

"I think it would be a good start if we were to begin by introducing ourselves, and explaining why we are here today," she said. It sounded just a little forbidding, and there was a moment of hesitation as the five students looked at each other. Then a man cleared his throat.

"Ok, I'll get us started," he said. "I'm Mitchell. I'm Canadian. I'm forty-eight years old. I work in law enforcement, and my hobby is that I try every year to get over here to Europe and learn a bit more about ancient civilisations. I've done a number of courses like this one, in different places."

Eva smiled and said, "Thank you, Mitchell." Mitchell adjusted his round, rimless glasses, and nodded seriously. Next to him was a dazzlingly pretty young woman with long blonde hair brushed back into a ponytail.

"I'm Ellie," she said. "I'm a freelance travel journalist, and I'm writing a feature on Italian art courses for a New York website. I want to be able to tell people everything about this course here in Rome, so I'll want to know all the details – where people are staying, where their favourite coffee shop is... everything." She beamed. "I think this is going to be great. I'm so looking forward to it."

The woman next to her was probably in her late thirties. She had a smile which looked as if it could easily edge into hostility, Dan thought, and honey-coloured eyes which also, somehow, looked dangerous. She gestured to the man sitting next to her. He was wearing a baseball cap and sitting back listlessly in his chair.

"I'm Dell," she said, "and this is my husband, Todd. We're American, and we're here on honeymoon." There was a little, friendly ripple, which she stilled. "Or rather, I should say, second honeymoon. We've been through some difficult times, no point denying it, but we've come through stronger, and more committed to supporting each other in our life journey." She paused, and there was another, slightly uncertain ripple. "It's been my dream to come to Rome and learn about the city and the art ever since I saw To Rome With Love. Todd knows it's my dream, and so... here we are." She took hold of Todd's hand.

"Thank you, Dell," Eva said. "And thank you, Todd."

And so it was his turn.

He said, "Hi, I'm Dan, I'm from London, and I've always been... interested in art." It sounded a bit limp, he thought.

But Eva smiled nonetheless, and said, "Well, I'd like to welcome you all to this course. The structure, as you know from your programme, is that we will meet here each morning for lectures and tutorials, and spend the afternoons in the galleries and museums of Rome. Obviously, we'll look at what we have here in the Museo di Roma, but we will also visit many of the great collections during the course, as well as public statues and monuments, and churches, and there will be scope to revisit anywhere that particularly interests you. So, if you would open your handouts at pages one and two…"

That afternoon, Dan walked back to his hotel slowly, by way of the river, taking pictures as he went, and realised that he'd barely thought about work all day. There was a message – no, there were two messages – from Jack, but he wasn't going to read them. He was on holiday. He was entitled to a holiday. He entered the hotel, and then remembered the unresolved suite/room issue, and once again approached the reception desk. The same young man as the evening before beamed at him, and then switched his smile off in order to listen intently.

"Please be assured, Mr Taylor, that everything is in order," he said. He obviously thought that Dan was some sort of insecure neurotic. "The suite is booked and paid for, and it is yours. No-one else's." He gently headed off Dan's further, ineffectual protest. "And will you be dining with us tonight, Mr Taylor?" he indicated the screen. "Dinner is of course incluso."

Over dinner – an extremely nice, and probably pretty expensive, dinner, which included aubergines and tagliatelle in a creamy sauce – he thought about the suite. It obviously belonged to someone, but that someone wasn't here, whereas he was. If that someone turned up, then he'd happily move out. He'd twice, no, three times, tried to let the hotel know there had been a mistake, so it wasn't as if he was trying to do anything fraudulent. And they could hardly charge him when they'd more or less insisted that he stay there. So after dinner he returned there, settled down in a linen-covered, oversized armchair, and did some more course reading. Tomorrow they were going to start to look at the Greek roots of Roman art. Fantastic. He had failed to notice the smartly-dressed man who stood casually by the reception desk, phone in hand, as he went past.

Chapter Five

"I just love him, don't you?" Dell murmured, as they both gazed at the Fighter. He sat, two thousand years old, a life-sized bronze, showing the marks of the contest on his face. He was physically powerful and defiant, and also powerless. Dan nodded. He had taken twenty, perhaps thirty, photos of the Fighter, and was still held by his presence.

Dell said, "Would you?" and he took a snap of her, smiling her menacing smile, alongside the statue. "Thanks," she said. "Shall I take one of you?"

"No thanks," he said. "I just want to... look a little longer."

"He certainly is something," she said thoughtfully, showing no signs of leaving him. "But not quite as something as his buddy back there." She nodded towards the previous room, where a larger-than-life nude athlete dominated the space. "Don't you think?" she added.

Dan smiled, now willing her to go away. He wasn't sure how well the second honeymoon was going. Todd was already in a nearby bar, having his first beer of the afternoon, and Dell had declined to join him. "I can drink beer back home," she had hissed. "I did not come all the way to Rome to drink beer."

Mitchell spotted them, and sauntered over with a wave.

"Aren't these guys something?" Dell said, indicating the Fighter.

"They certainly are," Mitchell said. "And vegetarian. It just goes to show."

"No, really?" Dell shook her head. "Isn't that amazing? They cared about animals way back then..." Mitchell was a natural conversationalist, happy to step into any breach. He also seemed to genuinely enjoy talking to Dell, and so Dan, spared from holding up his end of the conversation, took another photograph.

Ellie was already outside, consulting her laptop as to where they should go for their aperitivo. She had explained on the first day that she hoped to find a different venue for each evening, and to get everyone to score each of them on her matrix. Aperitivo was the early evening drink which was served with various snacks. The scoring included price, ambience, service, quality of drink, friendliness of staff (a different category from simple service), generosity and freshness of food, ability to speak English, cleanliness of bathroom, location and view. Tonight she was considering a rooftop bar which was potentially a little pricey, but which offered views over St Peter's and the river.

Dan was happy to be swept along with Ellie's general enthusiasm. Such had been his frame of mind when he booked this course that it hadn't occurred to him that there would be other people involved, and that he would be spending quite a lot of time with them. In many ways this was good – it was nice to be part of a small tribe in this big, alien city – but in other ways he needed a little more peace and quiet than he was getting. He wondered if he could excuse himself and just go for a walk. Todd had already given up on the aperitivo idea in favour of plain beer, and Mitchell preferred straight bourbon.

"Typical guys," Ellie had said, with her dazzling smile, shaking her head. "I guess it's down to us to actually try the drinks." She, he and Dell were therefore what Ellie called "the tasting panel." Even so…

"I'm so sorry you've got a headache," Ellie said, real concern in her voice. "Would you like some painkillers? They're good, and non-allergenic".

"I'll call Todd," Dell said decisively. "He can walk you back – it's dark out there now."

Dan thanked them, but said there was no need. Really. No need.

"At least take these," Mitchell said, handing him his own laminated large-scale map of the city and hiking water bottle.

"And phone us if you need anything, okay?" Ellie added.

Dan walked through the city for a long time, a tiny figure in the bustling evening. He paused from time to time to admire buildings and take photographs, and he wove through the crowds feeling himself as invisible and inconsequential as a drifting dandelion seed. It was a curious sensation, to be so completely free of responsibility. He walked back along the river, and skirted past a couple deep in a kiss. Quite a lot of kissing, and hugging, and holding hands seemed to go on in Rome. He would ignore it. He concentrated on finding his way to the bridge lined with statues of the Apostles, where he took some atmospheric night-time shots. He stopped at a small trattoria for a pizza and a beer, and then continued his long walk home. He didn't notice the businessman who strolled behind him.

Chapter Six

Daniel rubbed his eyes and put Francesco Loggi's work aside. The Russian was right – it was long, and useful as background, but there wasn't much in it that he could use. It had been common Roman practice, Loggi had explained, for a ring to be broken after the owner's death, to prevent the possibility of fraud, but Diocletian's ring had been given by his widow to the Church. It became a minor sensation, as its touch, or even just the sight of it, was said to cure blindness, deafness, lameness and barrenness. At some point it was transferred to Rome, where St Sebastian's body had been re-interred, and it remained in the Vatican. From the beginning it was a source of income, as the wealthy and ill of the city paid to venerate it. St Sebastian, meanwhile, was credited with stopping a terrible pestilence in the city in AD680, and worship of him grew. And during the plague times of the fourteenth century, when a third of the population died, the ring had become literally a touchstone. Loggi had unearthed partial records of the time, including reference to a merchant who had paid most of his fortune in order to touch the ring nine times – once for himself, once for his wife, and once for each of his seven children. But as the threat of plague receded, the ring faded in importance until it was finally taken off public display.

And now... Neither its theft from the Vatican in the early years of the nineteenth century, nor its use by Carlo III of Parma at his coronation in 1849, were likely to have much bearing on its present whereabouts. Daniel could see why the Russian had run out of patience.

He took a taxi from the airport, and finally was home. His flat was a spacious basement apartment that looked out on gardens at the front, and blank walls at the back. His office had a view only of the bricks – he found it helpful to gaze at them, to note the odd small discoloration, and the gaps in the cement, and to trace the patterns that ran vertically, horizontally, and diagonally. He threw his bag into a corner.

Before he began work, he made a brief note of the kestrel he had spotted on his journey from the airport. His habit of noticing and identifying birds had begun when he was thirteen. Then, he had been careful and methodical in his descriptions. Over time, the entries had become briefer and less frequent until they had more or less petered out. But even now, he still made a note if he saw something that lifted his spirits – like an elegant, high kestrel hovering in the cloudy London sky. He was a regular contributor to the RSPB, but he wasn't a member. Daniel had never joined any organisation, of any kind. It was unthinkable that he would join one to which a million other people belonged. He put his notebook away, and then made coffee and settled down at his desk.

He came closest to being at peace when he was working. It was when the cloud of irritation and tension which so often hovered over him would lift, for at least some of the time. It was always a relief to have a problem to work on which he could probably solve. His dreams, too, would become less troubled. And so Daniel was content to tolerate the Russian as a client, and to do his best to find the ring of Diocletian.

Chapter Seven

"Mrs Morris, Dan."

"What about her?" Why had he answered his phone?

"She was back at my surgery yesterday, with her yappy dog, saying that she's had no response from us. No letter, nothing."

"What's on her file?"

"Well, if I knew where her bloody file was, I wouldn't need to call you…"

"It's in the filing cabinet, Jack, under the letter M. M for Morris."

"There's no need to take that tone with me, Dan. Just tell me what date you wrote to her."

"Jack, I'm in Rome. How am I supposed to know what date I wrote to her?"

"You haven't got an internet connection?"

"Tell her I'll contact her once I'm back in the office."

"Excuse me – I think you're forgetting who works for whom in this situation. I'm the MP, and I'm the one she wants a reply from."

"Then why don't you reply?"

"Because I pay you to reply. My job is in Parliament, Dan, not pissing about in the office."

"Well, I'm on leave, Jack. Ask Lucy to look for her file."

"If I do that, she'll probably bring a complaint of sexual discrimination against me. She's a stroppy little madam."

"Jack, my beer's arrived. I have to go now."

"Dan, I'm warning you – don't you even think about hanging up on me…"

But he already had. He was sitting at a table outside a bar in a square surrounded by grand old apartment blocks, their stone lit by the soft evening sun. When occasionally a heavy front door opened, he caught glimpses of greenery in an interior courtyard, and broad marble staircases. What buildings. He contemplated, and then sipped, his Italian lager, while a high, white sky gradually took on shades of palest yellow and violet, and people chatted, and smoked, and relaxed at the end of the day.

Dan sat back, and briefly imagined what it would be like to live here. To saunter home from work, let himself into an old, magnificent apartment, pour a beer, sit on his balcony, and watch the evening unfold. There were no rules that said he had to live in London and work for Jack. None at all.

Chapter Eight

The phone call had interrupted him as he headed for the British Library.

"Yes?" he barked.

At the other end the Russian said, "Daniel? Why aren't you at home? And why aren't you using the secure phone?"

"How do you know I'm not at home?" Daniel asked, striding across the road, irritably dodging a taxi.

"I'm calling you there. You're not answering."

"And how can I help you?"

"I'm just interested in progress, Daniel."

"Well, when I have progress I'll let you know. As we agreed. Now I need to get on…"

"I thought we could have a little chat. A progress report."

"Sorry – I'm not at home and I'm busy. I'll be in touch when I've got news."

He was finally in sight of the library. He had already had to deal with one of the Russian's London contacts: a character called Emil who said he had a background as a private investigator, and could work with him.

"Our mutual friend wants you to have all the help you need," he'd said, draining his bottle of lager, as they'd stood in a crowded, early-evening pub. Daniel had noted the shaving rash on his bobbing Adam's apple, and his slicked-back thinning hair. He really did look like a private investigator – pinched for money, gaunt, and intense.

"Thanks, Emil," Daniel had said. "If I need you I'll call you." As he left, he added, "And don't follow me."

But he was pretty sure that Emil had done, and quite possibly still was. He wouldn't have been surprised to see his distinctive figure disappearing around a corner in Rome, or his muddy eyes peering up from an Italian newspaper.

Daniel's criteria for accepting work were fairly arbitrary. If a project looked difficult, and possibly interesting, then it was probably for him. Not much else was relevant. He had found the small drawing by Picasso which had been stolen from an exhibition in Chicago, the will that established the disputed ownership of a castle in southern Ireland, the sapphire bequeathed by a nineteenth-century Maharaja to his illegitimate daughter, the original plans of Tokyo's underground rail system. He was happy to be paid solely a finder's fee, and he required anonymity.

It was, he would acknowledge, an unusual way of life. It stemmed from two different sources. The first was that he considered himself to be probably unemployable. The concept of being told by someone else what to do – still less being given set hours in which to do it – was unthinkable. Impossible. He had survived his schooldays only by holding on to the knowledge that they would pass. And the second was his temperament. He remembered discovering Rubik's cube as a child, and falling in love with it. He had practised obsessively, using just one hand, and alternating right with left. It had seemed to him a metaphor for… everything, really. A fundamental order which underlay apparent chaos, and which could be summoned by persistence and intellect. He'd learnt, of course, that this was illusory – chaos always underlies apparent order, and could break through at any time. But he had a drive to resolve and to restore, and he'd found work that suited him perfectly.

Of course, not everything lost could be found again. But his experience was that things tended not to disappear so much as to just sink out of view. The ring could be in the hands of a private collector, or lying overlooked and miscatalogued in a museum somewhere, or be being quietly venerated at an altar to St Sebastian in some small, dark church.

He began by a process of elimination, skimming through the catalogues and sales reports of all the major auction houses going back sixty years, relying on his prospector's intuition to find the small note, the tiny clue that could open up the trail. He planned to spend the next few evenings following up Francesco Loggi's references, and reading all there was to know about the ring and its history.

It was dusk when he keyed in the code to the front door of his building. As he did so, a man approached him. Young, a little shaky, dark hair and stubble.

"Mr Taylor?"

Daniel paused. "And you are…?"

"My name is Sabato."

Bitten nails, a faint but distinct smell of tobacco.

"What do you want, Sabato?"

"I want to talk to you."

"About?"

"About the ring of Diocletian." He met Daniel's eyes and waited.

Daniel considered him. "Okay," he said finally. "Go to the Green Lion pub. It's at the far end of this road. There are tables outside. I'll meet you there in ten minutes."

"I'd rather—"

"If you want to talk, that's where we talk."

Daniel pushed the door, and it swung silently shut behind him. It was possible that the man had some useful information. It was also possible, and more likely, that he didn't. He peeled some money off a roll to take with him, just in case.

It wasn't a cold evening, but Sabato was wearing a heavy jumper, and a jacket, and a scarf. He looked tired. Daniel sat down on the opposite side of the slatted wooden table.

"Tell me," he said in Italian.

Sabato said cautiously, "I have information. I know something about the ring."

Daniel considered him. "Okay. First tell me something about you."

"What shall I tell you?"

"Who you are, how you know about me, how you know about the ring. How you got your information, what it is, and how much you want for it."

Sabato smiled wanly, shrugged and nodded. "Okay. But I

need a drink first."

"Fine." Daniel stood up. "What do you want?"

"I don't think I can get grappa here?"

Daniel shook his head.

"A brandy, then," Sabato said. "A double. A large one."

When Daniel returned, with a brandy for the Italian and a vodka for himself, Sabato had rolled and lit a cigarette. He sipped his drink and said, "My name is Sabato Iorio. I'm a researcher in history at the University of South Milan."

Daniel raised an eyebrow.

Sabato nodded. "Yes. It's where Francesco Loggi worked. I was a graduate student of his, and his research assistant."

Daniel watched the young man take a drag on his ravelling cigarette. He waited.

"I was there when the Russian first contacted him. Francesco had just published an article on the cult of the ring, and the Russian had somehow heard about it." He glanced at Daniel. "I guess he told you he wants it for his collection?"

Daniel nodded. "He made a point of it."

Sabato nodded. "Well, partly it's true, but he wouldn't want it so badly if Lorenzo Silvestri didn't want it."

Daniel had heard of Silvestri. He was chairman of Silvestri Enterprises, a large and often controversial multinational company. Silvestri himself, the grandson of the founder, featured frequently in the media. He would defend the Corporation's practices, attack his enemies, and pour scorn on his critics. He issued statements and didn't answer questions. He was particularly contemptuous of the Russian.

"And Lorenzo Silvestri wants it because he knows the Russian wants it," Sabato said. "Plus there's a rumour that one of Silvestri's grandchildren has an incurable skin condition." He smiled. "Incredible, no? He's a twenty-first-century billionaire, and he wants to invest in the power of St Sebastian." He fell silent for a few moments, and then said, "And Francesco got mixed up in it all. I don't know why he agreed to work for the Russian, but he did. Money, I guess. Francesco always lived a bit beyond his means. And I was working with him, so I was close to what was happening."

Another silence.

"What did happen?" Daniel asked.

"Francesco started getting threats about what would happen if he gave the ring to the Russian."

"From whom?"

Sabato shook his head. "They were signed 'The Defenders of Italy,' but that doesn't mean anything. There are all sorts of crazies on the far right. I don't even know how they'd found out about the Russian. Francesco thought..." Sabato hesitated.

"What did he think?"

"Well, we have a colleague called Mario Scipione. He's a twentieth-century specialist. Francesco's era, and mine, is the late Roman, so we didn't really have much to do with each other, but his office was next door to Francesco's, and he's... He's kind of a weird guy. Very bright, but politically very nationalist... I'm not sure that he's a fascist, exactly, but he's very close to that."

"Isn't that a problem at the University?"

Sabato smiled faintly.

"No. He has connections." He took a deep sip of his drink. "So, maybe Mario was involved some way, but he's a pretty secretive guy, and we didn't have any concrete evidence. But the threats got worse, and Francesco's tyres were getting slashed. I said he should just stop. Pull out of the deal with the Russian. Why not? At first Francesco wouldn't. He was quite a... proud person. He would have thought it was belittling to be intimidated by a few thugs. But, gradually, as the threats became more serious, and his windows started to get broken, he got frightened. He told the Russian he was going to stop, but... You know what the Russian's like. The man's a crazy himself. He told Francesco that he should be more frightened of breaking his agreement." Sabato's eyes met Daniel's. "I was going through all this with Francesco. It was an impossible situation. He was being threatened if he found the ring, and threatened if he didn't. What could he do?"

Misty rain had begun to fall, and the other tables were now

empty. Light poured from the windows, casting Sabato's face into deep shadow. Daniel swirled his glass, watching the last of the ice melting.

"We decided that he had to keep looking for the ring, but not find it," Sabato said. "I helped him. We wrote every week, adding to the report. Enough to keep the Russian quiet, not enough to bring more trouble to Francesco. A bit like Scheherazade, I suppose. The story of the ring is a very long one, after all." He shrugged. "In the end, the Russian gave up, and sacked him. That should have been good, and the end of all his troubles, but…" He shivered.

'But…?'

Sabato's voice, already low, sank to little more than a whisper.

"I found him dead. I'd just come back from a trip to the States. I'd been away four, five days. He was on the floor of his apartment. He'd been shot."

Daniel considered this. "Do you know who killed him?"

Sabato shook his head. "The whole place had been ransacked, pulled apart, but the police didn't find anything. I called the Russian, but of course he didn't care. Half of Francesco's head had been blown away."

Daniel took their empty glasses, and got more drinks. "Did Francesco find the ring?" he asked.

Sabato shook his head. "He had some leads," he said.

"What do you want from me?" Daniel asked.

Sabato took a swig of brandy, and then looked at Daniel.

"Protection," he said.

Chapter Nine

The message was waiting for Dan when he got back to the hotel.

"A gentleman has left this card for you," the receptionist said. The card simply contained a handwritten phone number. Dan turned it over, but it was blank.

"Did he leave a name?" he asked, but the receptionist shook his head.

Dan's plan had been to have a bath and then go out and try one of Ellie's top twenty medium-priced restaurants. But when he got back to his suite, impelled by curiosity, he rang the number. The call was picked up on the first ring.

"Good evening, Mr Taylor."

"Hello? Who is this?" He felt somehow a little unnerved.

The voice at the other end, an Italian man's voice, said, "I'm speaking to you on behalf of Signor Silvestri. He's interested in having a conversation with you."

"I'm sorry, I don't know anyone by that name. If it's about the suite, the thing is that the hotel—"

"Please, Mr Taylor. You know what this is about."

"I'm sorry, but I don't. This is a mistake. I don't know him – you."

And Dan abruptly put the receiver down. There was something about the voice that he hadn't liked.

He showered and then left the hotel. He took with him his biography of Caravaggio, and his camera. He wanted to take a walk, and shake off the slightly spooked feeling that the odd phone call had given him. It was dark, with a hint of more rain in the air, and Dan found himself drawn to a brightly-lit Irish bar, where Italian staff were pulling pints of Guinness for American customers, and giant screens showed English football. He had had a sense, just a very vague sense, of someone whose steps had been matching his own. He had even glanced over his shoulder once or twice, pretending he was checking the street names above him, but he'd seen nothing and no-one.

He ordered a beer and took a table outside, where a few smokers sat, silent, wrapped up against the damp air, and a street vendor was packing up his display of beads. Occasional windows shone faintly in the huge, anonymous old buildings opposite the bar. Two girls walked past, eating gelato. A shopkeeper was rolling down his blind. Dan wished he had a friend in this city. He checked his phone, and there were two queries from Lucy. He replied, sending a couple of useful links for a constituent who was having problems with her pension, and asked her to arrange an appointment for her with him for when he was back in London.

The afterglow of the sunset was gone. He was, after all, a stranger here. When in the UK did he ever sit on his own outside a bar? Come to that, when in the UK did he ever drink Guinness? He opened his book, but the lights from the bar weren't strong enough for him to read. There was a roar from the inside – a goal had been scored. He sipped his drink. He didn't like being a foreigner. He didn't like getting phone calls he didn't understand. He didn't like not being able to speak the language, and he particularly didn't like euros. He found himself peering at them to check what they were, and this made him feel incompetent. Not that anyone back in the UK, or his brother, would ever know this. He was posting a steady stream of photos on Facebook under the heading "Amazing city, amazing time," as if he was just too busy being amazed to put more than four words together. Infantile? Shallow? Never.

Of course he'd been delighted that Sam was getting married and delighted to be his best man. It is, after all, what brothers are for. Sam was three years younger than him, and they had always got on well, as he remembered. He'd been thrilled when Sam went to Oxford, thrilled when he got his doctorate, thrilled when he became one of the youngest-ever professors at Harvard, and particularly thrilled when he married a rich and glamorous photographer from a prestigious Boston family. A shame, of course, that Dan couldn't stay on for a little while. Their parents were having a holiday in Cape Cod, at a house owned by the parents of their new daughter-in-law, who were charming and generous people. But there it was – he had a plane to catch. Busy person. Busy European person, with art to go and look at.

The difference between him and Sam? Simply the difference that success makes. Confidence. The knowledge that you don't have to put up with some ridiculous job working for some ridiculous fool like Jack just in order to pay the rent on a ridiculous cupboard not even on a Tube line.

Dan strolled moodily back to his hotel. Once there, he was ushered to his table in the warmly glowing dining room. This soothed him a little. Here, everyone spoke English, and he wasn't a foreigner, he was a valued guest. He ate a very nice salad, made apparently with fennel, and a perfect fillet of fish with small potatoes and green beans. There was some sort of piano music playing in the background, and a peaceful, rising murmur from the other diners who filled the spacious room. A glass of white wine? Yes, why not? The elderly couple at the next table smiled at him, and he smiled back. After a very good coffee, he made his way back to his suite. From there he could see the outline of the Colosseum, floodlit and even more stern than by daylight. He gazed out at the lights of the city for a while, and then put on his reading lamp and settled down with Caravaggio. The phone lurked besides his chair, but it didn't ring again.

The next morning, Ellie explained her dilemma to Dan in a low voice while they sipped coffee in the overcast Piazza Navona. This was one of his favourite places in Rome. He watched a group of Asian tourists wearing ear-phones as they followed their guide around the perimeter, and a long crocodile of Italian schoolchildren, all scanning the surrounding buildings with their iPads as they marched past. At the café tables that lined the square, tourists and Romans drank coffee and looked out over the fountains and statues.

The atmosphere was relaxed and somehow celebratory, Dan felt, even in the gloomy morning.

"It's not just that the group is a bit too small to be an optimal learning experience," Ellie said. "Seven is really the ideal small-group number, and we've only got five. I know that's not Eva's fault, so I don't want to mark the course down just on that. I'll mention it, obviously, and suggest that people make sure they know how many people will be in the group before they sign up, but that's really... just..."

"Well, I think the course is very good," he said. "Excellent, in fact."

"Sure," Ellie said. "Sure. Certainly. In some ways, and for some people, it is excellent. But, on the matrix, it just isn't coming out very strongly."

"Really?"

Ellie nodded. "Eva is great, don't get me wrong, but she just isn't using IT the way it needs to be used these days. Where's the interactive white board?" She indicated their handouts. "Where are the graphics? Where are the links? Where is the interactivity?"

Dan was silent, a bit baffled.

"It's just so... flat," Ellie went on. "It doesn't do anything for people who learn visually."

"But we're here, in Rome, with the art to look at," he said, cautiously. He pointed to Bernini's Fountain of the Four Rivers, which stood in the centre of the Piazza, to illustrate his point. "Can't people learn visually from what we can... see?"

"Well..." Ellie said, and showed him the matrix on her computer. "It just could be better," she said gloomily. "I want to mention it to her, tactfully of course, so she knows how things are looking, but on the other hand I don't want to..." she lowered her voice to a whisper, "... skew the results. That's bad."

Dan didn't really know what to advise. As they strolled back to their lecture room he said, "Everyone is enjoying the course – even Dell and Todd. Shouldn't there be room for that in the matrix somewhere?"

And Ellie smiled and patted his arm, making him feel like a well-meaning but clueless uncle.

That was also the day that Mitchell had said to him, confidentially, "You know, if I didn't know better, I'd think we were being tailed."

"Tailed?"

Mitchell nodded. "When you work in law enforcement, you kind of develop an instinct." He frowned. "But... it's absurd, right?"

"Who would want to...?"

"Exactly," Mitchell said. "That's my point. We're just a bunch of tourists."

Dan would have preferred to think of himself as a visitor, but in general he agreed.

"Even so," Mitchell said, "you look at that guy over there..." He nodded towards a man standing by a newspaper stand, glancing casually over the magazines. To Dan, he looked like a perfectly ordinary man, and he would have completely discounted what Mitchell was saying, except that he still remembered, with an unease he couldn't fully explain, the phone call he'd received. So he nodded in a non-committal sort of way.

Mitchell said, "You know, this afternoon, I'm going to see if we can maybe split the group. Dell's told me that she's never been to the Colosseum. Well – you can't visit Rome, and not visit the Colosseum, can you?"

Dan considered Mitchell a brave man to even contemplate going anywhere with Dell. Todd was spending his days drinking and flirting with Ellie, and Dell's eyes seem to have turned the colour of dark ginger. Maybe Mitchell was trying to help, in his own way.

Ellie visibly brightened when she heard Mitchell's idea.

"An afternoon off would be great," she said. "And it demonstrates flexibility and sensitivity to the needs of the group – it will really lift the matrix. And I do need some time to go shopping," she added. "I can't compile a report on Rome without mentioning the Via del Corso."

Eva said, "Well, if it's just you and me this afternoon, Dan, we could go back to the Museo Nationale, and spend a little more time there. What do you think?" She smiled her slow, warm smile. Dan felt that she was far too nice for this bunch. They didn't deserve her. He was selfishly pleased that he could have what amounted to a private tutorial, and very glad indeed to spend some more time with Roman bronzes. They agreed to meet the others at a bar near the Colosseum later in the afternoon, and then headed off.

As they walked along the ancient winding street of Via del Governo Vecchio, weaving their way through tourists browsing shop windows, Eva explained how part of the building which housed the Museo Nationale had originally been part of the Baths of Diocletian.

"There had already been the enormous baths of Caracalla, out at Circo Massimo," she said. "But these were the biggest and grandest the city had ever seen. And they were named the Baths of Diocletian even though they were commissioned by a previous emperor and finished by a subsequent one. And even though Diocletian himself was never based in Rome... It's hard to take in their scale." She sketched with her hand a vast area, now a bus station and thoroughfare, which the baths had covered.

Difficult to imagine, and yet, in another way, it felt to Dan as if the Romans had never really left Rome. He had a sense of history somehow telescoped – as if the modern city was still cohabiting at some level with the citizens of two thousand years ago.

The trip to the Colosseum also, apparently, went well. Todd had had his photograph taken holding a pretend Roman sword to Dell's throat, and she had had a photo taken holding the same sword and threatening to run it through his guts. They sat around one of the tables on a terrace with a large umbrella shading them from the afternoon sun. The Colosseum glowered in the background while Segway riders sailed round it, vendors sold scarves and bags and keyrings, and pretend Centurions had their photos taken with tourists. Eva discussed the history of the Colosseum with Mitchell, and the cost of a photograph alongside a Roman soldier in full uniform (as opposed to a gladiator) with Ellie, and then, as they sat back and sipped beer, Mitchell said discreetly to Dan, "Well, I established something interesting today."

"Oh?"

"Whoever they are, Dan – they aren't interested in us."

"They?"

"The guys who've been watching us. They didn't come down to the Colosseum. That was the point of the separate trips – to see who they'd follow." His voice, already low, dropped further. "The person they're interested in is Eva."

Dan's heart sank a little. He said, "Mitchell, Eva's an academic and a museum curator. And she lives here. Why would anyone want…?"

Mitchell nodded. "Exactly, Dan. Who knows? She's involved with priceless antiquities. She has access to everything in the museum. Who knows what's going on here? The point is that we're foreigners, Dan. We don't know the first thing about what goes on in this city. Who knows what Eva is mixed up in…?"

Dan just shook his head. He couldn't even pretend to believe what Mitchell was saying. The Canadian shrugged. "Well, this is just a word to the wise," he said. "I'm keeping my eyes wide open, and I suggest you do too."

As the first beer became a second, and people started discussing restaurants, Dan realised that this was the evening they were all going to go out to dinner, to mark the end of their first week in Rome, and the halfway point in the course. Ellie had come up with a place that specialised in swordfish, spoke English, and was in a central part of the city, with panoramic views. Dan considered his options. He could plead a headache, again, or a toothache, and quietly escape back to his hotel. But that would mean leaving Eva to contend not only with Dell and Todd, but also Mitchell, and Ellie's matrix. And so, with the rather chilly Rome evening now surrounding them, they left the bar and headed across town to the restaurant. Everyone was fairly cheerful, and Dan began to think, cautiously, that the evening could be okay after all. He did hear Mitchell say, "Well, here's our friend again," as he nodded towards a man at a fruit stall on the opposite side of the road, but he pretended that he hadn't.

They found the restaurant, and settled themselves around the table. Todd and Dell sat next each other, the better to snipe, Mitchell sat next to Ellie, the better to explain his conspiracy theories, and Dan sat next to Eva, with Mitchell on his other side. Red wine, beer for Todd, and a conversation about the best and worst meals they'd ever eaten away from home.

"Don't ask Todd," Dell said, smiling her smile.

Todd turned slowly to look at her. "Why not?" he said. "Why not ask me?"

"Really?" Dell said. "You want them to know about the catfish?"

Todd said "Very funny, Dell. Ha ha."

"The thing about this catfish—" Dell had begun, when Mitchell said,

"You know, that reminds me of the first time I visited London. Has anyone tried fish and chips?"

Dan defended the national dish, and more wine was ordered. Was Italian bread as good as Canadian bread? Or better? Why couldn't Americans cook pasta like Italians? Why weren't all Italians fat?

Ellie explained her friendliness chart to Todd – which their waiter was doing very well on, by making eye contact and smiling – and Dell ordered everyone another limoncello. Dan, despite being next to Mitchell, was beginning to feel the wave of warmth and good fellowship that told him he'd had too much to drink. He leaned back and sipped his liqueur and was about to finally start a meaningful conversation with Eva, when Dell moved in decisively between him and Mitchell, and leaned her shoulder against his. When he moved his shoulder slightly out of her way, hers simply followed.

"How's it going, Dan?" she asked him, tilting her head to look at him.

"Okay," he said. "How about you?"

"Fine," she said. "Fine." She leaned back, so that now her

head was resting slightly against him. Dan didn't like this. He wasn't very sure what to do.

"Honeymoons, you know..." she said absently.

Dan nodded, as though this made some kind of sense, and in a way which he hoped headed off any further conversation. And luckily Mitchell was there.

"Over-rated?" he asked, raising a good-natured eyebrow.

"For sure," Dell said. Her eyes were watching Todd as he helped Ellie to do something on her computer. She turned her head lazily to look at Mitchell. "You married?" she asked.

"Divorced," Mitchell said.

"Smart guy," Dell said. "How about you, Dan? You married?"

He shook his head.

"Another smart guy," Dell said. "Let's have another drink."

Dan said, "Not for me, thanks, Dell." He realised, from the mildly outraged look he received, that probably the only way he could not drink more was to go. Even that would be a bit tricky. He stood up, slowly, so that Dell had time to move her head, and rest it instead against Mitchell.

"You're not going?" she said.

He nodded. "I..."

"Another headache?" Ellie asked concernedly.

"No, no, I..." He couldn't think of anything to say, so he just kept moving, mumbling something that sounded a bit like "medication."

"Oh..." Dell said. As he headed away from the table, he could hear her saying, "It's probably diabetes. Diabetics always need to take medication after meals. Poor Dan..."

"I didn't realise," he heard Eva say, and then he was out, and taking a long route back to his hotel. He felt gloomy and inadequate, a hangover already beginning to form behind his eyes. He walked past restaurants full of people laughing and not having to put up with Dell, past couples strolling, past successful people having successful evenings. The difference between him and Sam was intelligence. Not the academic sort – he had some of that – but the kind that had led his brother to make ambitious decisions, make useful connections, apply for prestigious jobs... Dan had never quite worked hard enough, because he'd never been quite sure of what he wanted to do, where he wanted to be, who he wanted to be... He hadn't even been a rebel. He'd just drifted. Just... drifted.

After his long, unhappy, meandering walk, he was grateful to let himself in to his spacious suite and gently collapse onto the bed. He didn't notice the man with the phone who passed him as he entered the lift.

Chapter Ten

Long after his conversation with Sabato, Daniel was awake. He sat propped by pillows, the screen of his laptop ticking away the hours of the night. Insomnia was an occupational hazard. He had toyed with the idea of going out for a run to help himself to think, but outside the night glittered with frost, and he had decided to wait until morning. Instead he spent time checking and cross-checking his classifications of all found references to the ring of Diocletian, otherwise known as the ring of Sebastian, within the past thirty years.

There were very few, until several years ago, when Mario Scipione, at a time when he was not yet employed by the University, had launched a fierce campaign in a nationalist magazine. Scipione was incensed by Italy's failure to treasure its heritage. This was exemplified by the lack of reverence for the ring of Diocletian – an indictment of those in power who, in his view, had sold out to craven political correctness. Daniel read through Mario's various articles and editorials, while mulling over his conversation with Sabato. His initial view had been that, basically, Sabato had nothing to offer him.

He had told him this – the long, rambling report on the ring was simply background reading. Sabato, after some hesitation, had said, "I also have Francesco's research materials."

"I've already seen his notes."

"No. The Russian doesn't have all of them."

"Why not?"

"He would have seen how close he was to finding the ring."

Daniel had sat back and sipped his drink. "Tell me," he said.

The key, Sabato said, was Mussolini.

They sat on in the darkening evening while the Italian rolled another cigarette and explained how the Roman Catholic Church, having finally managed to reclaim the ring from the Dukes of Parma and place it reverently in a shrine to St Sebastian, had then lost it to the Fascist leader when he achieved power. Il Duce had decided that he wanted to use the ring as Diocletian had used it nearly two thousand years earlier – as a symbol of authority, and for the sealing of documents and orders. He had kept it for the twenty-three years of his undisputed rule, and there were photographs of it on his chunky index finger. He'd used it to seal the death warrants of his enemies.

"It only disappeared when he was forced to leave Rome in 1943," Sabato said. "That's where the search begins."

And so Daniel lay awake, and tried to decide what to do next. On some level, he knew that he should probably rethink this whole job. His predecessor was dead, Sabato was badly scared, and his client hadn't troubled to mention any of this to him when they'd met. But, so much of what Daniel did came down to avoidance strategy – in particular the avoidance of tedium – that the heightened odds were, on the whole, welcome. Like a game player, he relished the chance to test his skills.

He looked again at the book Sabato had left with him, a thin hardback published in New York in 1949. An American Soldier's War in Italy had a frontispiece showing the author in uniform – a young man, fair hair slicked back, sceptical pale eyes looking straight forward, head held erect. Eric Littler had been born and raised in the town of Aberdeen, in Washington State, and had joined the American army in 1944, at the age of eighteen. The book was his recollection of the American Fifth Army's campaign through Italy, and its entry into Milan in April 1945, together with his photographs.

Eric Littler had already been a keen photographer when he signed up, and had taken every opportunity to record the army's progress. He had heard about, but hadn't witnessed,

Mussolini's flight from the city and subsequent execution. Somehow – he didn't quite explain how – he gained entry to the villa where Mussolini had been living for the latter part of the war, and had taken a series of pictures. Some of these had subsequently appeared in American magazines. A sharp young man. The photographs were mainly of grand, silent rooms and perfectly-made beds. Villa Feltrinelli, which had been confiscated from the Feltrinelli family for Mussolini's use, had since become a five-star hotel. There were two pictures of the dictator's bedroom which had interested Francesco. In the first, a pocket watch and chain, two rings and a pair of heavy gold cufflinks were clearly visible reflected in the large dressing-table mirror. In the second, a leather jewellery case could be seen inside a just-open drawer. There was no caption to either of the photographs.

Eric Littler was still alive, and still living in Aberdeen. Sabato said he had called him, since his English was better than Francesco's.

"It was possible," he explained, "that the Americans had just walked away and left the jewellery, but not very likely, so we thought Eric Littler could be a good contact."

"What did he say when you called?"

"I didn't actually speak to him, I spoke to his daughter. She was quite polite, but she said Eric didn't take calls from strangers." He met Daniel's unimpressed gaze. "It's a lead," he said. "Maybe a good lead."

Well, maybe. Maybe also a red herring, which Daniel really didn't have time for.

But... What if some enterprising young GI had brought the ring back to the USA in 1945? He pondered while he flicked through Mussolini's family tree, which included the politician Alessandra, and came across the interesting, though irrelevant, fact that her father Romano – Mussolini's youngest son – had played with what had been one of Italy's most popular jazz bands, The Romano Mussolini All Stars.

"I could come with you," Sabato had said quickly. "His daughter knows me. Kind of."

Finally, at four in the morning, Daniel checked flights.

Chapter Eleven

It was difficult to be exact. There wasn't any specific thing which had woken him, more a very slight sense that something was... what? In the darkness of his palatial bedroom, Dan instinctively lay still while he was tried to figure out why he was awake, and feeling somehow disturbed. Had it been a dream of some sort? He was about to slide back into sleep when he suddenly realised what it was... a very, very faint scent of tobacco smoke which had wafted briefly into his room from the balcony.

He froze. It was his balcony. No-one should be there. No-one could be there. He tried to convince himself that he was imagining things and tried to close his eyes again, but his senses were now all alert. He was wide awake. His room was on the seventh floor and his door had been locked. Therefore, no-one could have entered his suite. Therefore, no-one could have entered his bedroom. Therefore, no-one could be on his balcony.

Dan hesitated. If he got out of bed, if he put on the light, then he would be conceding the possibility that someone... that someone... And then he heard the faintest, faintest scuffing sound – the sound that a shoe makes when it crushes a cigarette. So slight a sound that he might easily have imagined it, but he knew beyond any doubt that he hadn't. His heart began to pound.

Finally, reluctantly, he eased himself out of bed, holding his breath, and tiptoed over to the French windows which led onto the balcony. He had left them slightly open, and now a night breeze caused their long net curtains to tremble. He edged slowly towards the gap, and then stopped. He could see a man's leg. A leg crossed over another leg, belonging to someone who was sitting in one of the balcony's large wicker chairs, and out of Dan's line of vision.

Dan was shaking a little, and utterly uncertain as to what to do next. Call security? Run? Demand to know what the man was doing there? And while he hesitated, the man stood up, moved towards the doors, and stepped casually inside.

"Mr Taylor – you're awake," he said. "An early riser."

He was calm and middle-aged, wearing a well-cut suit and a white shirt with a sober green tie. He had cropped grey hair and pleasant hazel eyes. Dan, who was wearing only a pair of boxers, backed away.

"I'm calling security," he said, in what he hoped was a warning kind of way but which possibly sounded more like a bleat. "I want you out of my room. Right now."

The man didn't show any sign of moving. He glanced at his watch.

"It's probably a little early for us to leave," he said. "You have time for a shower, or a shave, if you'd like one."

Dan began to wonder if he was having some kind of ultra-realistic dream. "What are you talking about?" he asked. "What are you doing here? Who the fuck are you?"

The man frowned just slightly. "Please, Mr Taylor," he said, and Dan recognised the voice.

"You phoned me," he said accusingly. "And now you're... harassing me. This is a criminal offence. I hope you know that."

The man said, "Mr Silvestri simply wants to have a conversation with you, Mr Taylor. It won't take long, or disturb the rest of your day."

Dan decided that his next move should be to get some clothes on. He pulled on the jeans and teeshirt he'd been wearing the day before, and then, feeling slightly more like himself, said, "I have no idea who you are, or who Mr Silvestri is. None. I've no intention of talking to him, or to you. You've already disturbed my bloody day. If you don't leave, I'll have you arrested. Get out of my bloody room."

The man now looked regretful. "I don't want to have to insist, Mr Taylor. Please co-operate. We need to have a civilised conversation."

It was then that Dan noticed the slight bulge in the pocket of his jacket. Sweet Jesus, he thought. He's got a gun.

In the silence that followed the man said, "Shall we go, Mr Taylor?" and made a gesture in the direction of the door.

They didn't speak on the journey. The limousine's windows were tinted, and Dan had no idea of direction as they sped along the early morning autostrada. They were leaving Rome behind. When finally the car drew to a halt, it was outside the back doors of a huge house. He glimpsed shrubs and trees. The sky was a pre-dawn grey, and he briefly heard the first birdsong of the morning as he was escorted into a hallway; the sound cut off as the door closed behind him. He was led along several corridors and finally into a large office. It had a faint scent of leather and wax polish. It was so dimly lit that it took him some time to make out the two figures sitting side by side at the top of a large oval glass conference table. He was shown to a seat on one side. The figures were a silver-haired man and a woman wearing sunglasses.

The man nodded and said, "Good morning, Mr Taylor. I am a great believer that the morning hours are the best hours of the day."

He had a clear, authoritative voice and spoke English with a slight American accent. He was possibly in his late sixties, with a small, neat goatee beard. He was impeccably dressed, despite the hour of the morning. His eyes, behind tortoiseshell glasses, were almost friendly. Almost, but not quite.

He said, "I am aware that you speak Italian. My English, also, is reasonably strong. However, for clarity, I have asked my interpreter to be here this morning." He then spoke rapidly in Italian, and the woman said,

"My interpreter is visually impaired. She sees very little. She needs low lighting, and it is for this reason that our lighting is not brighter. I trust it is comfortable for you."

Dan cleared his throat. The curious sensation that he was in a dream had been recurring from time to time throughout the morning, and it was especially strong now.

"I don't speak Italian," he said. Before he could say more, the interpreter had repeated his words in Italian, and the man had shrugged and smiled.

"As you wish, Mr Taylor. In which case it is even more fortunate that we have an interpreter present."

Dan said, "There's been a mistake. Of some sort."

The man spoke, and then the woman addressed the space at the end of the table. "There is no mistake, Mr Taylor. We have been aware of you from the outset."

"Outset? Outset of what?"

"Please, Mr Taylor. We don't need to waste each other's time. We've watched you as you have gone about your work. What is that English phrase? Hiding in plain sight? Well, now the time has come for us to speak." The words were delivered in the woman's bell-clear voice, her face turned just slightly towards him. Her accent was unplaceable. "The Russian's piracy stops here. Here and now. Is that clear to you?"

Dan said wearily, "I'm sorry. I have no idea what you're talking about. I'm a visitor here…"

The man leaned forward. He said, "You know who I am, Mr Taylor. Whatever fee you have agreed with the Russian, I will double it. Without question, without hesitation. Provided that you bring the ring to me. Just do that, Mr Taylor. Bring the ring to me."

"I don't…"

The man silenced him with a raised hand. He said tersely, "Let me be quite clear with you, Mr Taylor. You are in my country, in my city, seeking to rob me of something which belongs here. Here. And all to feed the vanity of a fool. Don't do that, Mr Taylor. That, believe me, is an extraordinarily dangerous thing to do. Be wise. Bring the ring to me."

That was it. The man and the woman stood up, and Dan was quickly and firmly escorted back to the car by the man in the green tie, who drove him through the steadily-building morning traffic and back to his hotel. They travelled in silence. It was still only eight o'clock when they arrived at the front doors. The man in the green tie waited, engine running, while he got out, and then the car slid away again.

Dan watched it go. He went upstairs and sat down on the floor, pulled his luxurious quilt from the bed and wrapped it around himself. He sat, still and stiff, while the morning replayed itself in his head.

What to do? What the hell to do?

Chapter Twelve

Aberdeen stood on a ribbon of road which ran for a thousand miles in each direction. The hire car had unpleasantly fuzzy seat covers and a very faint but unmistakeable smell of dogs. They drove in silence. Daniel had forbidden Sabato to smoke, or listen to the radio, or to drive, and so the Italian mainly slumped and gazed out of the window. Daniel kept his foot down and a wary eye on the temperature gauge, which was rising. It was this which in the end persuaded him to stop at a roadside McDonald's so that Sabato could buy a burger and coffee.

"Imagine," Sabato said, glancing around them. "Imagine coming from here to Italy." He winced at the coffee, but drank it. "And imagine coming back again."

The house was large, shabby, and surrounded by scrub grass. Sabato knocked on the screen door, and a woman in her sixties, white hair in a ponytail, opened the inner door and regarded them through the screen.

"Yes?" she said.

Sabato moved forward, smiling a warm, warm smile.

"Mrs Babington? It's Sabato Iorio. We spoke on the phone, about your father and his book. We said we'd come and visit, if it was permissible, and perhaps talk to your father about his memories."

"You're Italian," the woman said.

Sabato nodded. "Yes, I am," he confirmed.

"I'm afraid my father doesn't like Italians," the woman said. "Never has."

There was a silence for a few moments, while wind blew a few scattered leaves across their feet.

"My friend is British," Sabato said at last, gesturing to Daniel.

The woman didn't look impressed.

"Well, I'll ask him," she said, "but I don't think he's going to want to talk to you." She disappeared, and they stood and waited.

"It'll be okay," Sabato said. "She'll let us in."

Daniel said nothing.

When the woman returned, she said, with an air of finality, "He's asleep right now."

Sabato said, "That's fine, Mrs Babington. We can go and... have a coffee..."

The woman considered this. "Nearest coffee shop's fifty miles away."

"Oh."

She turned to Daniel. "What did you say your name was?"

"I'm Daniel Taylor," he said.

The woman said, "Well, I'm sorry you've had a wasted trip."

Then Sabato said, "It would have been good for my friend to speak to your father, because his father fought in Italy as well. At the same time. He was with the British Eighth."

"The British were there?"

He nodded.

The woman said, "Well, that's interesting." She hesitated. "I'll go and... but I'm afraid I don't think he's going to..."

She disappeared again. A middle-aged man washing his car on the other side of the road, slowly circling a soapy cloth on the windscreen, watched as they stood and waited some more. Cloud drifted across the high, white sky, and somewhere a dog was barking. Daniel and Sabato did not look at each other.

Time passed. Daniel watched a bird hovering overhead. A hawk. Swainson's hawk? Or a Ferruginous? It was too far away to tell. Finally, the woman came back. Her face was inscrutable, but when she spoke, it was with a crisp nod.

"Okay," she said. "You can come in." And the screen door swung open.

Eric Littler sat near to an electric heater, the TV remote control at his elbow. He was bright-eyed, with a thatch of white hair, dressed in a plaid shirt and a pair of corduroy trousers. He still had the tough, sceptical expression of his youth. He nodded to Daniel and Sabato as they came and sat down on the two dining chairs which Mrs Babington had placed for them on the other side of the heater.

"So you two have come from Italy?" he said.

"We've come from London," Daniel said.

"But you're Italian, right?" he asked.

"I'm Italian," Sabato admitted, "but he's British." He nodded at Daniel.

The room had wide windows that looked out over the sparse backyard. A large dresser stood between the windows, heaped with cameras and lenses and cases. The walls were lined with framed black-and-white photographs, and a collection of family portraits stood on the narrow mantelpiece.

Eric regarded Sabato. "I didn't like Italy," he said. "Didn't like the Italians. Didn't like Mussolini." He leaned forward. "And you may smile, young man. You don't know what things were like back then." He rubbed his hand across his forehead. "I don't really want to talk about the war," he said. "It was a bad time, and bad things happened. I haven't thought about those days for a long time."

"I've read your book," Daniel said, but Eric shook his head impatiently. "That... I wrote that to show my photographs," he said. "And it worked. I got a job on the paper here in Aberdeen, and I took photographs for the rest of my career. What do you think of that?" He peered at Daniel. "Didn't you say your dad fought in Italy?"

"He did," Sabato confirmed. "We wondered..."

"You look a bit young to have had your old man in the war," Eric said.

Sabato looked expectantly at Daniel, and when he hesitated, said, "His father married quite late in life."

"And he was with the Eighth?" Eric asked.

Daniel nodded.

"Well, those boys were there," Eric said grudgingly. "But the heavy lifting... That was us."

He looked again at Sabato. "It was chaos," he said. "Confusion. There were Americans, Germans, British, Italian fascists, Italian partisans, mobs of civilians..." He ruminated for a few moments. "I felt as though I'd walked into an alligator swamp. That's how it felt. Everything was... volatile. Unpredictable. Vicious. And we were young then, really young." He looked at Daniel. "Maybe your dad told you. So the book... It wasn't the whole story. It was just some pictures. And it made my family proud."

The sound of the dog barking was still faintly audible.

Daniel said, "You managed to get some photographs at Villa Feltrinelli."

Eric nodded slowly. "A few of us went over there," he said. "It was eerie, a whole palace just abandoned. There was one maid there, a girl of maybe sixteen, seventeen. She was terrified. We found her hiding." He cleared his throat. "Me, I'd just come to get some pictures, and that's what I did. This was war, you know."

"You took some pictures of Mussolini's bedroom... His things were still in there."

"Everything was still there. Shirts in the closet, shoes on a rack, jackets on hangers. Just as if he was going to come back any minute."

"There were things on the dressing table – a watch, and cufflinks, and rings."

Eric nodded.

"Do you know what happened to them, in the end?" Daniel asked.

"I don't know," Eric said. "I guess the boys would have taken them if they'd found them, but I don't know if they got as far as the bedrooms. I don't think they did." He shook his head, and his eyes briefly closed. "I didn't stay. After the girl, you know, I just wanted to get out of there. I wanted to get away." He glared at Sabato. "You can't possibly imagine. This was... brutal. Lawless. Mussolini..." He stopped. "You know, after he was shot, the Italians strung his body up. Italian people did that. We drove over and saw it. Right there, in the middle of the square, in front of a garage. All these bodies, dead, upside down. You can't imagine. His mistress... They'd tied her skirt at the knees, so it didn't fall down over her head. I noticed that. The crowd jeering and spitting at them, other bodies just sprawled there on the ground. I'd never... never seen anything like it. In the end, our boys put a stop to it. The bodies got taken down and buried."

Daniel said, "Mussolini had a ring which he'd taken from the Church."

"Doesn't surprise me."

"I wonder if you remember seeing it at the Villa?"

He handed him a sketch of the ring, but Eric, after peering at it, shook his head.

"I don't remember it," he said. "I'd like to have seen it – it sure is fine looking. There were a couple of men's rings, but I think they were plain gold. I don't remember anything with a stone. But I wasn't really paying attention."

"Okay," Daniel said. "Thank you very much for your time."

"Sure." Eric waved away their thanks. "Stay and have some tea," he said. "Jeanette knows how to make English tea. She'll be glad of a chance to practice."

They drank strong tea, and looked at the pictures along the walls. Eric had recorded local fairs and beauty pageants, college graduations and football matches. Jeanette picked up a framed picture of a young man, not very dissimilar to Eric, in military uniform, from the mantelpiece.

"This is Martin," she said. "My nephew. We lost him in Afghanistan six years ago now." She looked at Sabato. "You have a look of him. He had a really sweet smile." She glanced over at Eric. "Don't you think he's got a look of Martin?"

Eric shrugged. "Maybe. Martin was fair, though."

"Yes, but he had the same sort of smile." She put the photograph back.

"We need to go," Daniel said. "Thanks for the tea."

Father and daughter both nodded.

"Come back again," Jeanette said. "Any time. You'll be

welcome."

Daniel started the car, and they began the long journey back.

Chapter Thirteen

Dan, still wrapped in his quilt, was on his laptop looking for flights out of Rome. This wasn't panic – this was a rational response to an irrational situation. He had started by looking for flights to London, but realised that anywhere would do. He could fly to Frankfurt, or Paris, or Amsterdam, and then get a connection back. It might be better to do that, to throw Silvestri off his trail. He had to move quickly. This morning. He'd just go out, as if he was going to his class as usual, and not come back. He'd go to his class, in fact, and then leave and jump into a taxi. Which would mean that he couldn't take his case with him. He'd leave it. What did it matter? It was just a case. There was a flight to Vienna. Perfect. He was in the middle of booking when his phone rang and it was Jack.

He said, "Can't talk now, Jack. I've got a problem here."

Jack said, "Now listen, Dan, I think it's about time we straightened this whole thing out."

"What thing?"

"You know what thing. I was drunk, it was nothing, and it doesn't give you special rights to just take off whenever you feel like it..."

Dan sighed. He'd been drunk as well. Why else would he have let Jack snog him?

"Jack, I really can't talk now. I've got to go."

"I'm warning you, Dan, don't..."

He switched his phone off. Flight to Vienna, leaving at midday. Horribly expensive, but it had to be done. He put in his card details. This would make a great story one day in the future, he told himself. How he'd had to flee Rome because a famous industrialist had threatened him. Possibly backed by the Mafia, who could say?

That was it. Flight confirmed.

He thought about the Sistine Chapel, which they were due to visit later in the course. He'd had a poster of The Creation of Adam on his wall since he was sixteen. Whenever he'd moved, it had moved with him. But… He just had to… go.

He made an effort to act normally. He showered, shaved, went down to breakfast. The hotel dining room in the morning was a warm and comforting place, full of the scent of hot chocolate and freshly-baked pastries and coffee, with bread, cheese, ham and conserves set out alongside bowls of fruit. He poured a glass of orange juice and helped himself to his favourite cornetto. It was a marmellata, filled with soft apricot jam. He sat down at his table to wait until it was time to go to class. He glanced round at his fellow diners, but they seemed the same, ever-changing mix of business people and couples, the odd American family, Japanese tourists. Despite himself, he checked his phone. In his pocket he had his wallet and his passport. Walk to class, leave class, taxi to airport, airport, flight. Keep it simple.

Eva smiled her warm smile as he entered the lecture room.

"Borromini today," she said. "I know you've been looking forward to this. I thought we might do a bike tour of his work this afternoon, if everyone feels up to it. We'll be able to see more that way."

"That sounds great," Dan said, sadly. He had been indeed been looking forward to this. Borromini, the great contemporary and rival of Bernini, whose work was scattered over the city, playing with perspective in astonishing, Renaissance ways. He sat down and opened his notebook.

Mitchell shuffled in, with a "Good morning, folks," looking a little rough, and subsided into his seat. Dan realised with a sudden sharp shock that Mitchell had actually been right all along. But… too late to tell him so. Dell and Todd also arrived, separately, Todd wearing an I Love Spaghetti teeshirt, and Dell wearing dark glasses.

It was time.

He said, "Eva, I'm sorry, I'm not feeling terribly well this morning. I think I might go and…"

"Oh dear." Eva's dark eyes rested on him. "Another

headache?"

He nodded.

"Could be dropping sugar levels," Dell said. "You need to watch out for that."

"Well, you go, Dan, of course. You look quite pale. Go and lie down for a while."

"Thanks. I will." He gave a short wave to them all, the only goodbye he could make, and headed for the door. The taxi was no problem. Of course a bus would have been about ten times cheaper, but this wasn't the time to count pennies. Silvestri, with his almost-friendly eyes, was simply terrifying.

His driver was a man of few words, and they wove through the traffic with what seemed to Dan hair-raising nonchalance. He realised that he hadn't even thrown a coin into the Trevi Fountain, to make sure he came back again. He hadn't even posted his postcards. Well, too late. He was at the airport, he'd found his departure gate, and he was in time for a last Italian coffee.

It was then that he heard a voice shouting "Dan! Dan! Over here!" and he looked over to see Ellie, beaming and waving at him across the crowded concourse. Again, he had an overwhelming sensation of being in a dream. He stopped dead in his tracks, and watched as she made her way over to him.

"Have they found it?" she asked.

Dan stared at her. "What?" he asked weakly.

"Mr Silvestri said you'd come to pick up a bag they'd lost. You know, they're actually obliged to get it to you, there was no need for you to make the journey."

"No," Dan said. "No, they... haven't. Ellie, you know Silvesti?"

"Dan, thanks to you." She gave him a sudden, hard hug. "You're such a dark horse – I had no idea you had such friends. He's giving me an interview, right now, this morning, and I just can't believe it. He's one of the most controversial industrialists in the world. I'll be able to place it with... anyone. Wall Street Journal, New York Times, Economist.

It's the break of a lifetime. But he said you'd come out to the airport, so we thought we'd collect you on the way."

And sure enough, standing at a distance, was the man with the green tie. He nodded to Dan.

Dan again felt complete indecision swamp him. Make a run for it? His bloody plane wasn't ready to board yet. Refuse to go? The man couldn't exactly shoot him in front of a whole airport of people, could he? Maybe he could. And in any case, there was Ellie. He opened his mouth, to begin to warn her.

But she simply took his arm, and said cheerfully, "Our car awaits. Our driver's name is Piero."

Dan felt close to tears. This was all impossible.

The man in the green tie came over to them. "We need to go," he said, and Ellie beamed, and they walked out of the airport to where the car was waiting.

Chapter Fourteen

Back in London, rain was falling. Daniel pulled up his collar and waited for a taxi. His intention was to get home, deal with his messages, sleep for two hours, and then get on with his work. He'd lost sixty hours. Sabato, who had been silent for most of their journey, said, "There was another possibility."

"What?"

"For the ring."

"Sabato, one wasted trip is enough."

The young man shrugged. Daniel knew he was being unfair – the Eric Littler connection had actually been good research, and worth checking. It was perfectly possible that this other line, whatever it was, would also be worth following up. On the other hand, he'd noticed the ease with which Sabato improvised on the truth.

As they continued to edge their way up the queue, behind a group of cheerful Australians, he finally muttered, "You better hadn't be Scheherazading me."

Sabato sighed, a sigh which indicated that he had spent a long, long time in Daniel's company.

"Francesco thought it was a good lead."

"Then why didn't he follow it up?"

"Because he got shot."

At last, their taxi.

"Then tell me," Daniel said.

"I need a place to stay for a little while," Sabato said. "A safe place."

Daniel had known this would be the deal.

"Just tell me," he said. He was vaguely aware that he probably seemed to Sabato to be distant, obsessive, and terse. It surprised him slightly that he actually was all these things.

He listened to him, trying to weigh up probabilities. The Russian had begun ringing him the minute their plane touched down, and now Daniel answered.

"What's Sabato Iorio doing with you?" the Russian asked.

"He's scared he'll get murdered the way Francesco Loggi was. He's looking for protection."

"You, Daniel, are under my protection," the Russian said. "You have nothing to worry about, wherever you go. But I'm offering Sabato Iorio nothing. You can tell him that. Francesco was dishonest."

"Well, he has information."

"You think he's trustworthy?"

"I don't know. Possibly. You don't think so?"

"Scared people tell lies, Daniel."

"We'll see. I'm going to go over to Rome."

"Fine. I'll have someone there to meet you."

"I don't want anyone to meet me."

"And to book you a hotel. A good hotel. Somewhere safe."

"I don't want a hotel."

"Of course you do, Daniel. Rome is a very strange place."

This was, he knew, another of the Russian's beliefs. There was no point in reminding him of how well he knew the city.

"Sophia will arrange things," the Russian said. "She's very efficient. And she'll meet you. I'll give her this number for you – only this number. And this is also the number the hotel will have for you. You need to be careful, Daniel."

And so it was that Daniel had found himself in the pink sunset of Rome's Termini station, walking away from Sophia. Meanwhile Sabato was camped out on an arrangement of cushions on his study floor, with the heating turned up to a wholly unfamiliar level. Daniel said, "I'll be back in two weeks." He had taken a last look around his flat and added, "And don't even think about smoking in here."

Chapter Fifteen

"Wow," Ellie whispered to Dan, taking a cup of coffee offered by a uniformed maid. "Sometime you must tell me how you know this guy."

They were in a spacious, sunny morning room overlooking a green courtyard. Large, semi-abstract paintings filled the walls, and the scent of coffee permeated the air. Sofas were placed around a low, square table which held bowls of black grapes, apricots and fresh figs, alongside rows of small, perfect breakfast pastries.

The man in the green tie came over and said, "Mr Silvestri won't keep you waiting long, Miss Scott. He wonders if perhaps he could have a quick word with you first, Mr Taylor…"

Dan had been planning what he would say all the way out to the villa, and the minute he entered the gloom of the boardroom and saw Silvestri and his interpreter waiting, he said, "You must listen to me. This is all a mistake. You've made a big mistake."

The interpreter inclined her head and turned to translate, but the man stopped her. His eyes now looked like hard little coffee beans.

"Mr Taylor," he said, "I find your conduct…" He spoke briefly to the interpreter, who nodded her understanding, and added, "Reprehensible."

"Reprehensible," Silvestri repeated crisply. "What kind of a man behaves like this?"

Dan said fiercely, "You need to listen to me."

"No, Mr Taylor." Silvestri stopped him with a single raised finger. "On the contrary. You need to listen to me. I am going to extend the hospitality of my villa to all of the participants with you on this… course. They will be my guests for twenty-four hours. Within that time, you will bring the ring to me."

"You can't do this. I don't know anything about a ring. I —"

Silvestri held up his hand in a gesture of utter distain.

"Our conversation is at an end. You now fully understand the situation. Please say goodbye to the young lady and leave. Return with the ring."

Dan perhaps should have thrown himself to the ground; raged, shouted, screamed. But he had the distinct impression that none of this would have made any difference. And he was British. He therefore just repeated, hopelessly, "This is a mistake. A mistake."

The interpreter's dark glasses turned towards him with what was possibly mild sympathy, but she didn't bother translating.

"So you're a friend of Lorenzo Silvestri," Eva said, when he arrived at the lecture room. There was no warmth in her dark eyes. She was the only person there – all the others were on their way by limousine to Silvestri's palace, thrilled by such unexpected generosity.

"No." Dan shook his head emphatically. "I'm not. I'm in trouble, Eva."

She held out two cards, written in Italian.

"Invitations to dinner at Silvestri's palazzo tonight," she said, resting her eyes on his. "Not an invitation that can be refused – his driver will pick us up and take us. These were delivered to my apartment, Dan. That is where my mother and my son live. So I would like you to now tell me who you really are."

"I'm…" Dan sank onto a chair. "I'm nobody. I'm… I'm a visitor. A foreigner." His phone rang, but he just switched it off. He couldn't talk to anybody. "I'm a visitor." His brain felt as though it was spinning without any purchase. "I don't know why any of this is happening. I'm being threatened…"

"We're all being threatened," Eva said sharply. "You've brought this trouble with you. Whoever you are, you aren't nobody."

"Eva, please believe me. I'm just a guy from London. I'd never met Silvestri, or even heard of him, until I came here."

Her face grew, if anything, colder.

"Lorenzo Silvestri," she said, "comes from a powerful family, and he's a completely ruthless man. His companies are notorious for the crimes they have committed and got away with. That's why his nickname used to be Il Lupo – the wolf. He gets what he wants. I suggest you give it to him, whatever it is, before this goes any further."

Dan said, "Don't you think I would, if I could?"

Wearily and wretchedly, he began to tell his story again.

Chapter Sixteen

"Please – could you just get out of the way?"

A larger-than-life nude portrait of a blonde woman reclining on midnight-blue velvet went past Daniel on the shoulders of two removal men, followed by the woman who was clearly the model. She was tall, swathed in scarlet, and she lost a flip-flop as she went down the steps that led from the front doors to where a large van stood waiting.

"Damn this damn business," she muttered, as she wriggled her foot back onto the shoe. "This is all too much."

Daniel could almost see Il Duce's face in hers – the wide nose, the sensual mouth. She was possibly about sixty, with expensive blonde hair and flawless teeth.

"Mr Taylor, I'm sorry. My niece mentioned that you were coming, but, as you can see…" She stood aside as men came down the steps carrying boxes and more paintings. "This is simply a nightmare."

"I'm very sorry. I can come back another time."

"No, this is Agnese's fault. It's very sweet, of course, that she's come to help, but you know what the young are like." Daniel found himself caught in the gaze of her blue eyes. "They don't think. This has all been so chaotic. You'd think, wouldn't you, that I'd at least be allowed some time to move out, make arrangements, organise things… But no. This is a vendetta, Mr Taylor. Rest assured." She paused as a young woman came out of the house – a shock of tousled Italian hair and a wide, Californian smile.

"Hi, Mr Taylor. Sabato said you'd be over. Have you met my aunt?"

"Livia," the woman in scarlet said, presenting her hand so that Daniel had the choice of shaking or kissing it. "I'm pleased to meet you," he said. "But I'm sorry this is bad timing."

"Well, maybe not," Agnese said. "Maybe you really can help us, Mr Taylor."

Daniel, quietly baffled, smiled and said, "Well, of course, I'd be happy to…"

Agnese said to Livia, "Sabato says that Mr Taylor works for a big auction house. A very important one, in England. And they want to put together a sale of World War Two memorabilia." She turned her wide, cornflower-blue eyes to him for confirmation.

Daniel cleared his throat and said, "Well, yes, kind of…"

"I have nothing," Livia said, bitterly. "Look. I'm being thrown out of my home. I've got to go and live with Alessandro. I know he's your father, Agnese, and my brother, but the man is intolerable. I'm sorry. I should just lie down here, on the steps, and die. That's what it's come to. That's what I should do."

Agnese said, "Why don't we go and have a cup of coffee? We don't need to be here. The men know what they're doing."

"You trust these men?" Livia said, incredulously. "You think my furniture will survive?"

Agnese said again, "I think it's worth talking to Mr Taylor. He might be able to help." She linked her arm encouragingly through her aunt's. "We'll be back in time to rescue the furniture. Let's just talk." She led the way down the drive, and along the quiet road to a piazza where there was a bar. They took a table in the window.

"I can't believe any of this," Livia said, desolately, munching a croissant and sipping cappuccino. "Such malice."

Agnese said, in a low voice, "There was a mortgage on the property. In the end there was nothing we could do…"

"I'm sorry," Daniel said.

"Well, that's why I thought it would be a good idea for you to talk to my aunt and my father, when Sabato told me about you," Agnese said. "I don't think very much came down to them, but I know they do have a few things. You could tell them how much they're worth. Maybe it could make a difference. I've lent them what I can, but we don't have enough to keep Livia's house."

"I'd certainly be interested in anything your family may have," Daniel said.

Sabato had made contact with Agnese, in the hope of speaking to Livia and Alessandro. He'd got on well with her, but then couldn't persuade either her father or aunt to speak to him. He told Daniel that Alessandro had moved to the States as a young man, and acted in a number of 1970s movies. It was while he was living briefly in Hollywood that he had met Agnese's mother, a Californian wine heiress, but things hadn't worked out between them, and in the end he had returned to Italy. Livia, in Rome, had made quite a grand marriage, which also hadn't worked out, and since then had been locked in a struggle with creditors – a struggle which, finally, she had lost.

"If the ring has stayed in the family, they'll know," Sabato had said. "And they're definitely the best ones to approach. They both need money."

Now Livia nodded sadly, and drummed long cerise fingernails against the saucer of her cup.

"We need something, God knows," she said. "I can't live with your father. Well, you know. You know him." She looked at Daniel. "But we got very little…"

"Well, I'd be very happy to look at anything you have," Daniel said blandly. "Or anything you may know of."

"Yes, but our politics are very different to his, and to a few others in our family," Livia said. "We're not apologists for fascism, Mr Taylor."

"Please, call me Daniel," he said.

Livia inclined her head graciously.

"A lot was lost," she said. "Lost, stolen, destroyed…"

"Well, if you can think of anything," Daniel said, handing her a card. "Anything at all." He rose. A look passed between Livia and her niece that he couldn't read.

Livia said, "You know, Daniel, we are invited to a birthday celebration this evening. Not that I can face it. And I'll be completely exhausted after today. But I'll probably go, and my brother will be there. Why don't you come? You'd be very welcome, and it might be a chance for us to... talk a little more."

"If you're sure, I'd be delighted," Daniel said.

"Good," Agnese said, and favoured him with her radiant smile. "That's a date."

Chapter Seventeen

"I'm always amused by Americans," Daniel's neighbour said, talking across him to the elderly man on his right. "Here's me in front of the Colosseum," she mimicked in a strong Italian accent, "here's me beside the Pantheon, here's me, here's me…" She chuckled, and took a sip of wine. The long table held twenty people, and waiting staff bustled in and out silently. The room was spacious, softly lit, with a marble floor and frescoed ceiling in the Renaissance style. Candles burned in tall silver holders that stood in a row along the centre of the table. The food was traditionally Roman, and stuffed zucchini blossoms gave way to gnocchi alla Romana, and porchetta.

"You've a good appetite," his neighbour said to him approvingly, as the plates were cleared. The guests were a mix of family and friends. The conversation swirled around the usual topics – the economy, the inadequacy of the government, and of Rome's administration, the way the city was being allowed to decay, numbers of foreigners, the impossibility of the bureaucracy, the corruption. Alessandro was sitting some way down the table on the opposite side to Daniel. He, too, resembled Benito – something in the eyes, and the mouth. He was a stocky, handsome man, who seemed to have an opinion on everything. Agnese, his daughter, listened, shook her head and smiled.

The reason for the dinner was the eightieth birthday of a friend of Livia's, a shrewd man called Fulvio who was an art dealer. He seemed unfazed by this great birthday – thin, impeccably dressed, with wispy white hair and horn-rimmed glasses. Daniel was consciously keeping some distance from him – he genuinely did know the world of auction houses, and he'd have a nose for deception.

After the birthday cake, a dark chocolate torte, had been handed around, and the last toast drunk, coffee was served. It was at this point that Alessandro strolled over to Daniel.

"I wonder if we could have a little chat?" he asked.

Daniel could see that he was just slightly drunk. "Absolutely," he said.

"Please." Alessandro gestured towards a door that led off the dining room, and Daniel found himself in a chilly, unused library. He took a seat and waited while Livia, Agnese and Alessandro dusted off leather armchairs and sat down.

"So," Alessandro said. "You're interested in Second World War memorabilia?"

Daniel nodded. Cautiously.

Livia leaned forward. "Is it correct, Daniel, that you would be interested in the ring of Diocletian?"

He cleared his throat. "Yes. I'd be very interested."

"Would it be worth much?"

He nodded. "It would be worth a great deal."

Livia said to Alessandro. "You see?" She sat back impatiently.

Alessandro shrugged, and a gloomy silence fell.

"Do you have this ring?" Daniel asked, at last.

"Yes," Livia said.

"No," Alessandro said, at the same time.

"Yes and no," Livia conceded.

"Family," Alessandro said, tersely. "And other considerations."

"But the ring is valuable?" Livia asked.

Daniel nodded. "Potentially it's very valuable."

Livia said, "Daniel, thank you so much for coming this evening." She fixed Alessandro with her intense blue gaze. "We'll talk about it, and call you."

He chose to walk back into town, following the long, tree-lined road that swept down one of Rome's great hillsides. It was a mild night, illuminated by a half-moon surrounded by pale, lit cloud, and Daniel allowed himself to stroll, and listen to the cry of a hunting barn owl. Progress at last. He was sure of it.

Chapter Eighteen

Dan now had a real headache. However, he didn't feel able to complain. He sat in the back of the limousine, silent. He and Eva were being driven out to Silvestri's villa by the man in the green tie, with the radio tuned to a local Rome station. A phone-in was being aired, and a succession of meaningless voices, cheerful, angry, emphatic, reasonable, filtered through the car's speakers. Dan had been prone to migraine as a child, and he wondered if the stress of all this was going to bring one on for the first time in his adult life.

Eva sat some way away from him. She too was apparently thinking. She was completely still and calm. She had inclined her head in chilly thanks as the car door had been opened for her, and now she kept her face turned away from him, gazing at her reflection in the tinted windows.

Dan caught the words "Roma" and "Juventus"... Football? Was that what they were talking about? He felt as though he had somehow been dragged underwater. Life was continuing on the surface – people were chatting, traffic was moving – whereas he was locked into slow, suffocating pressure. He felt a sense of grievance that Eva hadn't believed him, and was no doubt silently blaming him for all of this. But possibly... possibly he'd feel the same if their positions were reversed. He slid around uncomfortably on the oxblood leather, cold in spite of the car's warmth, and tried, yet again, to figure out what to do.

The villa was decked out for the evening with twinkling lights and illuminated fountains. It was like a movie set, the scene where James Bond strolls in wearing a tuxedo, and the gorgeous girl smoking the cigarette glances up at him. Dan and Eva found their group comfortably ensconced in the morning room he'd visited – had it only been that morning? –

sipping apertivi and nibbling an array of crisps, nuts, and olives. He noticed that Ellie and Todd were once more sitting close together at her laptop, and that Mitchell and Dell were also deep in conversation. Everyone stood up when Dan and Eva entered, and Dan found himself being hugged by Ellie, again, and also by Dell, while Todd beamed at him, and even Mitchell looked pleased.

"This has been the most fantastic day," Ellie said. "I did the interview, oh my God, so interesting, and we've been able to look around the villa, and see Mr Silvestri's collections – Eva, you will just love his mosaics, some of them are from Pompeii, just unbelievable – and we've toured the gardens, and we've been so, so well looked after. Mr Silvestri has personally invited us to stay tonight, as his guests... It feels like a dream."

Eva smiled, a pale imitation of her usual warmth, and said, "Good. I'm glad you're enjoying your visit." She accepted a glass of water and a seat by the window, so that she could look out over the illuminated gardens.

Dan, hero of the hour, sipped a fruit juice. He couldn't drink – he needed to focus on getting everyone out of this situation. But, on the other hand, it seemed that they were going to be stuck there for the night whatever happened, so surely a small drink would do no harm?

"Wait till you see your rooms," Ellie said. "They're absolutely beautiful."

Dan wondered when Silvestri himself would put in an appearance. That would be his chance to finally convince him that he'd got things wrong. He'd brought his passport and he was going to insist that Silvestri look at it. He'd also call Jack, and get Jack to confirm who he was. It was all very well Eva looking at him like he'd crawled out from under a stone – none of this was his fault. None of it. Defiantly, he accepted a cocktail.

By the time they were ushered in to the dining room, a huge room lit with candles, Dan was beginning to feel just a little drowsy. No sign yet of Silvestri. Everyone was quiet, subdued slightly by the richness of their surroundings and by the absence of their host. Ellie had closed her laptop, having lost her internet connection.

"Funny – I thought he was going to be here," she said.

Was there a slight, growing puzzlement? A sense that all this was just slightly… odd?

But the food was impeccable, and Dell raised her glass and said, "Here's to us all, and here's to Mr Silvestri."

Everyone responded to the toast, and then got on with eating artichokes cooked with oil and herbs, and pasta in rich tomato and aubergine sauce.

Mitchell cheerfully raised his glass. "Here's to Rome." Again, glasses were lifted in response.

Dan wished that he could speak to Mitchell, but the Canadian was busy discussing the health benefits of the Mediterranean diet versus the Japanese diet with Dell, and Dan's sense of helplessness began to morph into a lethargy which was almost overwhelming. Eva, he noticed, barely touched her food, and Dan concentrated on repeating to himself, over and over, the words he was going to say to Silvestri. You've got the wrong man. Look at my passport. Talk to my MP. You have to let everyone go right now. Immediately.

After dinner, they returned to the morning room for coffee and liqueurs. And there, on one of the sofas, sat a tall priest. He was middle-aged, a rather stern figure, and he had seemingly just arrived, as his black travelling bag was on the floor beside him, his black coat draped over the handle.

Ellie smiled at him. "Buona sera, padre," she said.

The priest smiled and rose. "Good evening. I'm sorry I missed dinner."

"You're British," Ellie said.

The priest smiled again and nodded. "I'm attached to the Vatican, but I'm originally from the UK," he said. He shook hands with everyone, with the immaculate courtesy of a diplomat.

"And are you a friend of Mr Silvestri?" Ellie asked.

"No. I know of him, obviously. But the invitation this evening was because I understood that my brother was to be a guest here." He looked around the group, smiled and shrugged. "But clearly he hasn't made it. Rather typical of my brother."

At this moment the man in the green tie came in and murmured to Dan, "I wonder if you could come with me for a few moments."

Dan stood up, immediately completely wakeful and flooded with adrenalin.

"Of course," he said.

They walked in silence from the room, followed by curious eyes, and along corridors, through doors, up stairs, until finally they arrived back in the boardroom. This time, the lights were on and there was no interpreter present – just Silvestri himself, faultlessly dressed as always, sitting at the top of the table and waiting for Dan. As Dan moved forward, he was startled to see a door at the back of the room abruptly open, and two small curly-haired children peer in, before an adult hand gently drew them back and closed the door.

Silvestri, who had briefly glanced around, said, "My grandchildren, Mr Taylor. They're here for the weekend. Please sit down."

Dan, however, could not respond to either the children or to Silvestri, as his brain struggled through the stress and alcohol to articulate the speech he'd been rehearsing. Remaining on his feet, he said, "Mr Silvestri, we need to talk," like the hero of a Western confronting the villain in the town saloon. "Here's my passport." He dragged it out of his pocket. "Look at it."

"Please, Mr Taylor," Silvestri said coldly, holding up a hand to silence him. "I hope you understand now how completely serious I am. I had hoped you would realise that the time for games is over. But... as you please. Be aware, however, that you, your colleagues and your brother will remain as my guests here until such time as I receive the ring. My car and a driver are at your disposal. There is no phone signal. However, any calls you wish to make can be made on my landline. You need only to ask. Good evening, Mr Taylor."

And he stood up, withdrawing his eyes from Dan contemptuously, and strode through the door at the back of the room. Dan caught a brief sound of children's happy voices before the door closed.

"What are you talking about?" Dan said, to the empty room. "My brother is in Boston."

Chapter Nineteen

Daniel had expected a call by the next morning, but none had come. He rang Sabato, but only got his voicemail. He restlessly left his hotel, pausing while a long green tram rattled past him, and then crossed the road next to the Basilica, and headed down to the small bar near the market for coffee. He took a seat at an outside table, and then, seconds later, Sophia arrived. She smiled and took the other seat at the table. Despite himself, he was becoming impressed by her persistence. All around them, people were having breakfast on their way to work, and the staff behind the counter were producing espressos, cappuccinos and lattes with the rapid rhythm of a well-oiled machine – receipt on counter, saucer on counter, spoon on saucer, cup on saucer.

"Good morning," Sophia said. "Did you sleep well?" She was wearing a neatly tailored grey coat, and smelt of something floral… Iris.

"Very well, thank you," he said, although in fact he'd lain awake for most of the night listening to the city. He had begun to resign himself to the fact that, on most mornings, he was going to have his coffee with Sophia.

"Our client sends his regards to you," she said. "I spoke to him earlier. He hopes you're making progress."

"Excellent progress, thank you," Daniel replied, opening his paper.

Sophia smiled. "That's good to hear. After all, you only have… how long left?"

Daniel buried himself in the business section.

Sophia drained her cup and said serenely, "Have a good day, Daniel."

He watched her as she left the bar. He couldn't talk to her. He simply couldn't – it would allow his client even more scope to interfere. And besides... he worked best alone. He always had. She turned and gave him a brief wave, and then she was gone.

He had almost given up on the phone call when it came. He was by that time on the Metro, on his way to the huge city library.

"Mr Taylor?"

He pressed the phone to his ear, surrounded by the noise of a busy underground train.

"Yes, speaking."

The voice, he realised with surprise, was that of Agnese.

"I wonder if we could meet?"

"Of course," he said. "Where?"

"Do you know Il Palazzo delle Esposizioni?"

This was a huge gallery on Via Nationale. "Yes," he said.

"I'm there now," Agnese said. "I'll wait for you."

Daniel, who was travelling in the wrong direction, jumped off at the next stop, and headed back into the city centre.

Agnese was wrapped in a vast plaid scarf, looking like a petulant waif. She led him through the bookshop to a café which opened onto a courtyard, and ordered hot chocolate.

"There was a bit of a row last night after you left," she said. The sound of a rehearsing choir drifted in from the adjoining church, and sunlight flickered through the leaves of the overhanging trees. An elderly man at the next table leaned back and tranquilly exhaled smoke.

Agnese flapped her hands irritably. "Italy," she said, in English. "Honestly. This so wouldn't happen in California." She glared at the man, who didn't appear to notice.

"The problem is," she went on, "that we really do need the money. Well, I don't. I'm married to Julio, and things are fine for us." Daniel, in his insomniac research, had come across Agnese's widely-reported Hollywood wedding, to which every guest had been required to wear lavender. "But my father and my aunt, they're in dire straits. And we haven't got so much that we can really help them out much more. Not in a meaningful way. But they're not going to survive sharing a house. One of them is going to kill the other one. So it is definitely a good idea for them to get rid of the ring for whatever they can get for it."

She paused to stir cream into her cup of thick chocolate. "But my father has issues, because he doesn't want it to fall into the hands of neo-fascists, and that would be a risk. The far right haven't gone away in Italy. Well, you probably know that. So there's the question of how it could be sold at auction without being sold to them. Or to Lorenzo Silvestri."

Daniel raised an enquiring eyebrow. "Why wouldn't you want to sell to him?"

"Because we hate him," Agnese said simply. She sipped her drink. "And it isn't just my father and Livia who would have to agree. I have an uncle, Luca, over in England, and an aunt, who lives over here. She's a little…"

Daniel knew that she was referring to Mariaurora, the oldest of the four siblings, who had seemingly lived in seclusion since her twenties. The only information Sabato had been able to give him was that she was a founder of a charity devoted to supporting the work of the Church.

"She's crazy, to tell you the truth," Agnese said. "I haven't met her very often. She disapproves totally of Livia and my father, and they haven't spoken for years, but she kind of likes me. She sends me prayer cards and things. She's very… devout. She dresses kind of like a nun, although she isn't one, and lives in a kind of a… place." Agnese's vocabulary clearly didn't contain a word bad enough for where her aunt lived. "And she's got the ring. Well, it's in a bank, and she's got the key. She thinks the ring is a sacred trust from God."

"I see."

"She won't care about the situation the family is in. She's as completely selfish as my father in her own way. But, if we could get my father to agree, and if you could meet her and let her know that it's really valuable, we could maybe persuade her to let it go so she can do good with the money. With her share of it." She spooned in a little sugar, and slowly sank it into the chocolate. "Luca probably won't care what we do. We need to persuade my father, and Mariaurora."

Daniel said, "There is an interested buyer. He's Russian – a collector. He owns a bust of Diocletian, and he'd like to acquire the ring for his museum in St Petersburg."

"He isn't a fascist?"

"No, not as far as I know."

"Well." Agnese considered this, and nodded. "A museum in St Petersburg sounds okay," she said. "So it wouldn't need to go to auction?"

"No."

Agnese shrugged. "Okay. I'll let my father know. And after that… Mariaurora." She beamed and stood up. "I think we might be in business."

Chapter Twenty

Dan hadn't slept at all in his room at the palazzo. Each time his eyes had drifted shut, his brain had abruptly snapped them open again. At five in the morning, he was already up. The man in the green tie was also awake, relaxed and impeccably groomed.

"Good morning, Mr Taylor. Please come and take breakfast. And after that, the car is ready for you."

Dan muttered something indistinct, which might have been "Leave me alone," and shuffled into the morning room. The previous night's conversation with the priest, Father Julian Taylor, hadn't made him feel any better. He had fixed his slightly hooded pale eyes on Dan, and then rested his chin on his fingertips, as though analysing an interesting abstract problem.

"Of course, the difficulty is proving that there's no connection… You have the same name, nationality and age as my brother. You both have passports which describe your occupation as researcher." Dan had explained that he was actually a caseworker, and had only put researcher because he thought it sounded a little more professional, but the priest had merely continued, with a sigh, "You both live in London. It seems that you arrived in Rome on the same flight, and you're staying at the same hotel. Or should be. Only my brother, being my brother, isn't actually there."

"Who is your brother, exactly?" Dan had asked.

Julian had smiled and shrugged. "We're not in very regular contact. But Daniel has, it seems, has gained a reputation as a finder of objects which are difficult to find. I don't really know much about the detail of what he does. But I know that it's work which suits him very well. He enjoys challenge and he enjoys invisibility." He tapped his fingers together. "Which is part of the problem. He has a passport photo, of course, but apart from that I'm not aware that there's been any picture taken of my brother since he was fifteen."

"Can't you call him?" Dan had ventured, after a gloomy silence.

"I can possibly try tomorrow," the priest said. "There isn't any signal here at the moment. And meantime, I'll pray." He said this as if it was somehow useful. As he stood up, and stretched, he added, "We are, after all, in the hands of the Lord."

Now, Eva was in the morning room, also looking exhausted, nursing a cup of pale tea.

"Dan," she said quietly, "we have to do something. This situation can't go on. It's dangerous."

He nodded. He had never, in his whole life, felt quite as crap as he did now.

Eva said, "You have to get the ring to Silvestri. There's no choice in this."

"Eva, I have no idea how to do that. None. You heard what the priest said. This other Daniel Taylor, whoever he is, knows how to do it, but I don't."

Eva took a sip of her tea. She considered him. She finally said, "What if I could help you?"

"Really? Can you?"

"It might be possible." She put her cup down. There was a wary look in her eyes that he had never seen before. "If I thought that this was some sort of set-up, Dan, I would... mind. I would mind very much."

He shook his head, feeling as helpless and ineffectual as a stuffed bear. "Eva, do I look like I could have set all this up? Please?"

Her eyes didn't leave him. "Tell me, Dan," she said, "why did you come to Rome?"

Why? It all now seemed so long ago.

"I just wanted..." He shook his head. "I wanted to have seen it for myself..." He really didn't have more of an explanation than this. He'd booked the course, and the costly hotel, on a rainy Friday morning in late November. His latest relationship had fallen apart, and he'd moved out of their flat and into a truly miserable room. He had arrived at work late and drenched, having been almost knocked off his bike by a bus. It was the morning that he'd received his brother's wedding invitation. On the back, Sam had written, in pencil, Things will get better, bro. This was, of course, a thoughtful and brotherly message. It had filled him with a rage that could have devoured the whole world. Things will get better? Sod you. Sod you, Sam. So instead of dealing with the constituents' queries which were on his desk waiting for him, he had taken an hour to research and book this holiday. It had been a small but satisfying act of defiance.

"To have seen Michelangelo," he said.

Eva nodded absently, as though she recognised this. She was seemingly lost in thought. Dan waited. The man in the green tie waited. Finally she said, "Ok – let's get moving." She nodded to the man, whose name, he remembered, was Piero. "He is ready to go now," she said, in English. "And I will go with him."

Dan still hadn't actually had any coffee, let alone any breakfast, but he didn't bother to point this out. Just to get away from the villa would be something, even it was inside the claustrophobic car. Piero, a casually efficient chauffeur, led them out of the morning room, through the green courtyard, and into a second, wide enclosure which held garages and a number of parked cars. All huge, glossy, and Italian. The moon had faded, and the early morning was chilly, with dew shining on the dark stone flags under their feet. Dan briefly caught the scent of hyacinths, a whisper which was there and then gone, and the smell of wet, freshly-cut grass. Piero opened the door of the dark-glass limousine, and they climbed in. Eva had already told him an address, and they pulled smoothly away from the back of the villa, down the long drive, and onto the road. Eva sat upright, her hands folded, her eyes abstracted. She didn't look like she wanted to hold a conversation. But on the other hand…

"Eva," he finally asked, "where are we going?"

Chapter Twenty-One

"How does this make sense?" Alessandro had asked. "You say you work for an auction house, and then you say there's a private buyer..."

It didn't, of course, make sense. Daniel had mentally cursed Sabato, and hesitated. And Livia had stepped helpfully into the breach.

"I don't suppose it makes any difference to the auction house, does it?" she'd asked Daniel. "The commission will still be paid, I presume."

"Yes, that's right," Daniel had said. "It doesn't matter to us how the ring is sold."

Alessandro had been about to ask another question, but Livia cut him off impatiently. "Now come on," she said. "We need to get there and get this over with."

She was dressed in severe black, her hair swept back and pinned, the only flash of colour from her lipstick. Alessandro moodily finished his cigarette.

"There's no point us getting there before Agnese," he said.

"I've spoken to Agnese," Livia said. "She's already on her way. So we need to go."

She skirted the furniture and pictures which stood in the middle of Alessandro's wide, decrepit hallway. The jumble extended into one of the grand front rooms – a piano, suitcases, a wardrobe, several more large, naked canvases of Livia, stacks of black bin bags, an unplugged fridge. She gestured to it as she went past.

"How can we live like this? We can't. We have to sort this out with Mariaurora."

Alessandro reluctantly pulled on his leather jacket. "We just need to keep it short," he said.

"Absolutely," Livia said. "Short. And business-like."

They climbed into Alessandro's 1947 Buick, and drove slowly through central Rome, past the walls of the Vatican, past the dome of St Peter's, and along an inner-city autostrada out to where Mariaurora lived. Agnese met them on the corner of Mariaurora's building. It was a huge, ancient palazzo which now housed shops and bars on its ground floor, and offices on the upper floors. Agnese, too, was wearing black.

Alessandro said, "You'd better go first – you're the only one she'll be pleased to see." He then sounded one of the buzzers at the side of the huge, battered old door. "Mariaurora? It's us."

There was the buzz of an electronic lock being released, and Alessandro pushed the door open. Ahead of them, a long, poorly-lit corridor. On one side, a dingy lift; on the other, stairs which led down into darkness.

"We should take the stairs," Livia whispered. "I'm not risking that lift." Alessandro nodded, and they descended in single file: Agnese, then Alessandro, then Livia, and finally Daniel. There was an indefinable smell, composed of damp, some sort of rotting fruit, and (possibly) fish. Daniel could feel the temperature dropping as they went down. At the bottom of the stairs, Alessandro groped for a light switch, and at that moment Daniel's phone rang. An unknown number.

"Yes?"

"So I've finally got hold of you," a voice said. The reception was poor and crackly, and Daniel could barely make out what was being said. "When you get back, you can tell me just what the bloody hell you've been playing at."

Daniel said, "I'm sorry, who is this?"

"Don't come that with me, Dan. We need to talk."

Nobody ever called Daniel Dan. He said, "I think you have a wrong number," and snapped his phone off. He'd check on the caller later.

Alessandro had found the light, and they were now able to see a dark, featureless door in front of them. There was no bell.

"It stinks down here," Agnese muttered, while Alessandro

rapped on the door with his knuckle. There was then a long pause, and Daniel could see that Livia was beginning to shiver, in spite of her cashmere poncho. The door was finally opened by a tall, imperious woman who wore a thick, flowing grey wool robe and a grey scarf around her fading fair hair. Her feet were bare, the toes slightly purple with cold. She stood blocking the doorway while her chill eyes travelled over her visitors.

"A deputation," she said.

"Hardly," Alessandro said. "Are you going to let us in?"

She was unmistakably their sister – the same eyes and full lips, the same haughty bearing. She stood aside and they entered a vast room whose far walls were invisible in the gloom. She nodded curtly to all of them except Agnese, for whom there was a brief kiss. The floor was made of uneven, worn stone flags. A life-size crucifix was propped against the wall at the side of the door. A large, neon-lit picture of the Sacred Heart of Jesus hung alongside it. The lighting was a series of small, bare bulbs strung seemingly randomly across the ceiling, each creating a small pool of light in the room's shadows. There was a modern gas heater in the middle of the room, and several elderly chairs.

Without waiting to be invited, Alessandro walked over and sat down. The others followed, Livia brushing the seat with one of her gloves before she sat. Mariaurora remained standing. The chairs were surrounded by enormous, sliding heaps of newspapers and books, and huge drifts of flyers. Daniel guessed that Mariaurora distributed these. He caught glimpses of headlines: "He Is Risen!" and "Are You Ready?" Mariaurora's eyes fell on him.

"And this is the man you were talking about?" she asked.

Livia nodded. "This is Mr Taylor," she said. "He's British. He's an expert in valuing things."

Daniel rose, and put out his hand. "I'm very pleased to meet you," he said, but Mariaurora ignored him. She turned to her brother.

"I think you've wasted Mr Taylor's time, and your own," she said. "I have no intention of permitting the ring of St

Sebastian to fall into ungodly hands. And certainly not just to settle your and Livia's debts."

"Well, you can explain to me how you think the ring of St Sebastian is doing any good in the world while it's locked in a bank vault," Alessandro said. "Nothing very sacred about that, is there?"

He and his older sister stared at each other for a moment, a locking of steely blue eyes.

"It was God's will that the ring came to us," Mariaurora said. "It's held by us in trust. That is the will of the Lord. It isn't for us to question."

Alessandro laughed and raised his hands in a gesture of contemptuous helplessness. Mariaurora's face turned, if anything, paler.

Daniel said, "The person who is interested in the ring owns a museum. It would be safe there, and it would be visible. You could write a full history which could be displayed with it. Perhaps with a couple of your tracts. It might be responsible for... converting people."

Agnese said, carefully, "Maybe God has sent Mr Taylor to us, Aunt. Maybe it's God's will that the ring should go to the museum."

Livia, clearly impressed by Agnese's reasoning, nodded, and murmured piously, "Absolutely. God's will."

Mariaurora visibly hesitated, and was about to respond when something ran across Livia's feet and she screamed.

"Oh for pity's sake," Mariaurora said irritably. "It's only the cat. Daisy, come." And a large orange cat stalked from around the back of Livia's chair and rubbed herself against her owner's grey-clad legs. "You're in her chair," Mariaurora told Livia. It seemed that the moment had passed – Mariaurora and Livia were looking at each other with undisguised dislike – but again Agnese intervened.

"Aunt, we could all take a little time and go and pray. What do you think? Seek some guidance from the Lord."

"This is where I pray," Mariaurora said. "This is my church."

"Well, maybe you could pray here, and we could all

pray… somewhere else. And I could perhaps give you a call a little later on? Maybe this evening?"

Mariaurora inclined her stately head.

"If you wish," she said.

That was the end of the meeting. Back upstairs, in sunlight, Livia beat cat hairs off her poncho and shuddered.

"I'm so sorry you had to endure that, Mr Taylor," she said. "Our sister is a ghastly woman."

They retired to the bar of a hotel to recover. Livia joined Alessandro in a whisky, Agnese had a white wine, and Daniel a coffee. The good thing was that the family were now completely onside, and as committed as he was to the Russian buying the ring. The problem…

"The problem is timing," he said. "The Russian wants the ring quite quickly."

Agnese said, "Maybe I can call her back in an hour or so. And maybe Livia could try Luca again…?"

Livia nodded. "Yes. Just don't ask me to visit Mariaurora again."

Agnese said, "We might need to go back… But maybe not all of us…"

Livia raised her glass. "Bless you, bella. When we get the money, I'll buy you and Julio a holiday in Switzerland."

Agnese laughed. "When we get the money, I'll buy myself one." She turned to Daniel. "It may be that we can get things agreed this evening, then go to the bank tomorrow…" She looked at him with suddenly serious eyes. "It's possible… we could have the ring by tomorrow evening."

Chapter Twenty-Two

Eva said, "You have to understand what things were like here before the war. I don't know if you know very much of our history... Italy was terribly poor. Poorer than we can imagine now. It was trying to modernise, and it was under the control of a dictator who had made Parliament into a mockery. He created Fascism, and it was popular. It was optimistic."

The car was edging along a road of tall, dingy apartment blocks with graffitied walls, looking for a place to park. This was an area of warehouses, garages, and small shops, with nothing but more grey apartment blocks and tram lines as far as the eye could see. Eva and Dan had travelled in silence most of the way, but now she seemed to feel it important that he understand a few things.

"Of course it ended in disaster. But my grandmother... She knew Mussolini well. She worked in his office at Villa Torlonia. She was devoted to him. She believed he was the saviour of the country, and she still believes it. As far as she's concerned, the wrong side won."

Finally their vehicle double-parked, blocking in three other cars. Piero remained at the wheel as they climbed out. Dan followed Eva to the door of one of the anonymous blocks, and they took the narrow lift up to the tenth floor. A tiny, stern woman, glasses perched in her short silver hair, opened the door.

"Eva. Cara."

They embraced, talking in rapid Italian, and then Dan was shown into a living room. It had a tiled floor, with rugs spread out in front of the sofa, and photographs lining the sideboard and the windowsill. Dan could see pictures of family groups, the men sitting on chairs, the women standing and holding babies or toddlers, with bigger children sitting on the ground, cross-legged, beaming at the camera. There was a black-and-white picture of Eva's grandmother as a young woman, surprisingly like her granddaughter, with glossy hair and warm dark eyes. And there, next to the big Madonna, Dan saw a small picture which had been placed in a mother-of-pearl frame. The unmistakeable figure of Mussolini, in an open-neck shirt, smiling and relaxed, and next to him, looking proud and pleased, Eva's grandmother.

Her name, it transpired, was Claudia. She and Eva made coffee in the tiny kitchen, and brought it in on an ornate tray painted with big roses. Dan accepted his small cup. He couldn't get used to coffee that consisted of just a single mouthful. He liked his coffee by the mug. But... when in Rome. He was aware of being under Claudia's scrutiny, and he sipped.

Eva said, "My grandmother is very concerned about this situation. She thinks you have put all of us in danger."

"I..."

But she wasn't listening to him. Again, an exchange in Italian so rapid that it sounded like water flowing. Then Claudia indicated that she wished to speak to Dan, and Eva translated.

"My grandmother says that she will explain things to you." A slight sigh, while her grandmother spoke. "She says that Il Duce was betrayed – first by the Germans, and then by his own people." She added, quickly, "Not my view, of course." She paused while Claudia spoke. "When he was killed... She heard about it on the radio. She was here, in Rome. She went at once to Milan. It was very difficult to travel, but she got there. She wanted to see him. She also wanted to ensure that he was buried properly, in proper clothes, and wearing his medals and his rings. When she got to the Villa, there were American soldiers there. She had to wait until they'd gone. She knew that Il Duce had kept the ring of Diocletian in a pouch in the pocket of his general's jacket. The uniform was there in the wardrobe, and so was the ring. She couldn't find the wedding ring, and she thinks the Americans had stolen it. She put the uniform and the pouch into her case, and went into town. The Americans were in charge, and no-one would speak to her. She found out that he had already been buried. She was too late. She slept that night in the doorway of a shop, using the case as a pillow."

Claudia bowed her head. She spoke in a low voice, and Eva translated quietly. "No-one can imagine her grief. She wanted to die as well, and be buried next to him. She felt that the Italian nation had just gone completely insane. And the Americans... They were brutes. Arrogant, domineering brutes."

Claudia stopped and lifted her coffee cup, and Eva looked over at Dan.

"I remember my grandmother telling me this story when I was small," she said. "I remember her sleeping in a doorway with her case for a pillow."

Her grandmother spoke again, and Eva translated. "And so she went into a church, and asked the priest if she could leave these things with him. She didn't know what else to do – she couldn't travel back to Rome with them. He wasn't a fascist, but she thinks he felt sorry for her. And maybe scared, as well. He said that he'd put them up on top of the confessional. There was a space up there, and a façade, so they'd be hidden." She shrugged. "And that was the last my grandmother saw of them."

Dan felt as if he had stepped in to an odd play of some sort. His headache, low blood sugar, and the shot of caffeine he'd just drunk, combined to give him a curious sense of detachment. He watched as the small cups were loaded back onto the painted tray, and Eva carried them back into the kitchen. The rattling sound as they were put into the sink seemed to him preternaturally loud. Left alone under the gaze of the unrepentant, elderly fascist, he felt a wave of fatigue wash over him.

He gave what he knew was an inane smile. Had he been able to speak her language, he would probably have made an inane remark as well. She didn't smile back. He wondered why Eva had thought this visit would help. Even if Claudia's memory was reliable – which was not a given – it was hardly likely that the case containing the dictator's dress uniform and ring would have stayed on top of a random confessional box for over sixty years.

Eva returned to the living room.

Claudia spoke again, in her rapid way, and Eva said, "My grandmother said she had a visitor a little while ago. Someone from the University of South Milan, who was interested in Mussolini's last days." She pondered this. "I studied there – I still have friends in the History Department. Maybe we could pay a visit – check out the church where my grandmother left the case, and talk to my colleagues at the University."

Dan said, "It just seems... I don't know. A bit of a long shot."

Eva said, "Yes, I agree, Dan. But the other option is to go back and tell Lorenzo Silvestri that we've made no progress. Do you really want to do that? This way, we can at least show that we've done everything we could."

He nodded, trying not to look as hopeless as he felt. He wanted to tell Eva he was sorry, sorry for the whole stupid thing, but instead he said, "Okay. Let's go to Milan."

Chapter Twenty-Three

Agnese listened to her mobile, and nodded. "Yes, that's fine. That's fine, Aunt. We'll see you at seven-thirty... See you." She ended the call. "She says she's prayed, and she has a decision for us."

"What do you think?" Livia asked her. "What's she decided?"

"I don't know," Agnese said. "She says she just wants to see me and Daniel... I don't know if that's a good sign or not."

Daniel glanced at his watch. "How long will it take us to get there?" he asked.

"Not long," Agnese said, indifferently. "I'll drive."

They were sitting in the cold kitchen of Alessandro's house. He himself had gone out to buy more brandy.

Livia said, "If she says no, then we need to have a plan. I can't stay here. I simply can't." She gestured at the sink. "Look at it. Look at this place."

"Can't you kind of... outvote her?" Agnese asked. "You, my dad, and Luca?"

"I'm not sure Luca would be much help," Livia said. "You know what he's like – well, you don't, because we never hear from him. He's sulky, Luca. Always has been. But maybe myself and Alessandro could. It was left to all of us, after all." She sighed, a deep sigh. "Go and see her, Agnese. And you, Daniel. Persuade her. You'll be saving me from a fate worse than death."

Before they left, Daniel had a few minutes to check his calls. On the Russian's phone, the Russian, of course, and Sabato, wanting to know what was happening. First he called back the person who had addressed him as Dan. The phone sounded as if it was ringing far away, and the interference was, if anything, worse.

"Who are you?" he asked. "And how did you get this number?"

The person at the other end gave a snort of derisive laughter.

"That's fine, Dan, fine," he said. "I'm sure there's a reason why you've changed your phone, so I had to call your bloody hotel to get a number for you. It might even be a good reason. But the thing is... I don't care what that reason is, Dan. It isn't relevant. I don't give a toss. Is that clear? You've shot your bolt with me. Welcome to the world of job-seeking." And he hung up.

Daniel shook his head, and then deleted the call. Nonsense, whoever it was.

The Russian said, "You're getting some strange calls, Daniel. I'm looking in to it. And I don't know what you're thinking of – you're working with Sabato, who's as slippery as an eel, and not working with Sophia, who is solid as a stone. Is that correct in English, solid as a stone? She is, Daniel, and I expect you and her to work together in Rome..."

Sabato said, "If this doesn't work out, Daniel, there was another lead Francesco was working on..."

Daniel said, more sharply than he'd intended, "Let's just hope this does work out." He didn't add that he had no more time to waste, but that was true.

And, on his own phone, a message from a Father O'Brien at the Vatican. Daniel rang him.

"Mr Taylor," an American voice said. "Thanks for returning my call. It's just that your brother isn't here and isn't answering his phone. We thought you might know where he was."

Daniel frowned. "Why did you think I might know?"

"Well, he said he was going to meet you for dinner yesterday, when he got back from Cologne. Your number is in his diary."

"Really?" Daniel shifted the phone to his other ear, to be sure he was hearing correctly. "Do you know where he was going to meet me?"

"You were both invited to be guests at Lorenzo Silvestri's villa, I gather."

Daniel was baffled. He said, "If I hear from him, I'll certainly ask him to call you... Thank you for calling, Father. Let's hope he turns up soon."

It occurred to him after he had ended the call that this might have sounded a little casual. But he had no idea what Julian was up to, and therefore no idea what he should either say or do. His brother was deeply mysterious – older by nine years, distant as the moon. He tried calling him, but it went directly to voicemail.

"Julian, it's Daniel," he said. "Call me."

"Time to go," Agnese said. She was dressed purposefully in purple. "Mariaurora has just got to agree with us," she said, as they climbed into the car. "I need to get back to New Mexico, Livia needs to get away from my dad... It's all so inconvenient..." She switched the engine on. "And you're sure it's ok with the auction house if we just sell to this Russian?"

"It's fine," Daniel replied, a little absently.

"Good." Agnese looked at him with languorous, black-fringed eyes. "I'd hate it if you got in trouble with your boss." They pulled out into the slow stream of Rome's evening traffic, and crawled along despite Agnese's use of the horn and impatient overtaking manoeuvres.

"I hate the traffic in this city," she muttered, as she skirted around a bus, scattering motor scooters and causing several other cars to brake. "You just have to be... assertive."

As they continued to edge through the congestion, she said, "So, Daniel, what's your story?"

"Story?"

"Are you married? Divorced? In love? Heartbroken?" She flashed him her conspiratorial smile. "Still looking, maybe?"

Daniel smiled and shook his head. "No, none of those," he said.

"Then what?"

This wasn't an easy question to answer. The nearest he had

come to love had been a relationship with a young dancer called Mayya whom he'd met when he was in his twenties. They had shared the attic of a crumbling London house, and he'd learnt the Russian for "I love you," because Mayya had said it, often, but he had never quite said it back. Why? He didn't know. He'd been young. But he had a feeling that he'd still be the same now – too aware of the anguish of loss to put himself in its way. He had been, he was sure, impossible. He wasn't proud of himself. He and Mayya had quarrelled often, and hadn't parted well.

And so he shrugged and smiled again, and let the conversation lapse. Agnese looked at him, thoughtfully, and then turned her eyes to the road.

They arrived at last. Agnese unhesitatingly double-parked, slamming the car door behind her.

"Honestly. Rome," she sighed.

Then they were back in the dingy corridor, and descending the unlit stairs.

"We should have brought a torch," Agnese said. At the bottom, she found the light switch, and they were again in front of the dark door. This time, however, it was open by just a crack.

Agnese called, "Hello, Aunt," and she was about to push the door fully open, but some instinct made Daniel take hold of her arm.

"Wait," he said. "Wait just a minute..." He cautiously edged in to the room.

There had been no struggle. The furniture, books and flyers were all untouched. But lying on the floor, gazing sightlessly at the bulb in the ceiling above her, was Mariaurora. Dark blood was pooled around her head, and he could see the hole in her forehead where the bullet had entered. Her body was sprawled, as though she was stretching out to sleep.

Agnese had followed him in, and now she stood with her hands to her mouth saying, "Oh God. God. Oh God."

"Agnese, we need to get out of here." Daniel edged back towards the door, drawing her with him. She finally turned her gaze from her aunt's body towards him.

"We have to call the police."

He nodded. "Let's get up onto the street and do that. Come on."

He took her hand, and half pushed her up the staircase and along the corridor to the front door. The driver of the car double-parked by Agnese's Smart car was sounding his horn, there was a whirl of wind and a rush of laughing teenagers who passed like a flock of starlings. Daniel dialled the emergency number while Agnese stood and shivered beside him. The blocked-in driver wound his window down.

"Move! Move this bastard car! Move it!" He stared in outraged perplexity at the two unmoving figures on the pavement.

Daniel had just finished giving the address to the operator when he saw Sophia, as neat and upflappable as ever, crossing the road towards them. It was obvious that she knew what had happened.

"Daniel, the police had already received a report of shots being fired. They're on their way." She turned to Agnese. "Do you have the keys?" she asked. "I'll move your car."

Agnese mutely handed them over, and Sophia got into the Smart car and drove it away, giving the furious driver a serene finger as she did so. Daniel found himself glad of her calm presence.

Agnese said, "I feel sick. I think I'm going to be sick…" And she vomited against the side of the building. Daniel turned up his coat collar. The temperature had dropped, and the wind surged in gusts around the corner of the street. He knew that this evening was going to be interminable.

Agnese sat down on the steps in front of the building with her scarf wrapped around her face. Sophia came back, and sat down beside her and put an arm around her.

"I need to tell my family," Agnese said suddenly. "They don't know…" She found her phone and called Livia, but as soon as she tried to tell her what had happened, she started to cry. She handed the phone to Daniel.

"I'm afraid there's bad news, Livia," he said.

She listened, and let out a sharp gasp. "We'll be there," she said. "Tell Agnese we're on our way." She hung up, and Daniel handed the phone back.

It was after two in the morning when he finally signed his police statement and was free to go. He confirmed that he'd be available if the investigating detectives wanted to talk to him again. Agnese had already gone home with Livia and Alessandro. The detective who took his statement was a cool man in his forties whose general expression was that of kindly disbelief.

"You know," he said, "I have a feeling about you, Mr Taylor. I think that if it had just been you who found the body, and not Agnese, you might not have called the police." He raised quizzical light brown eyes to Daniel's. "Am I right? You might have just searched the room and gone. Left someone else to deal with... all this."

He quite possibly was right, but Daniel shook his head.

"I called you," he said, reasonably. "And I've done everything I can to assist."

The detective nodded acknowledgement. "True," he said. "We appreciate it." He glanced at his phone. "Okay, we'll call it a night."

Daniel fastened his coat. He decided to walk – a long, long walk around the city and along the river. He needed to think. Mariaurora's death had clearly been the work of a professional killer. It again raised the question of what exactly he was doing here. He left the police station, and almost walked past Sophia's green Fiat, in which she sat with the engine running and a jazz station playing.

"I told Emiliano to let me know when he'd finished with you," she said. "A drink?" she asked, glancing over at him as they pulled away into the empty road. He just nodded, and she said, "I know a place..."

They drove to a big, dignified hotel, close to the Villa Borghese, parked in a quiet side street, and entered the dimly-lit and almost deserted bar. Two middle-aged American men were talking baseball in a corner, and a bored young barman was polishing the counter. Rufus Wainwright was singing softly in the background.

"Ciao, Marco," Sophia said.

"Ciao, Sophia." He flipped the cloth in her direction. "For me, a brandy. For my friend, I think... a vodka?"

"Thanks," Daniel said. They took a table set back from the door, and the barman brought their drinks over. "Thanks, Sophia," Daniel said, raising his glass.

She said, "So... What now?"

He shook his head. "I don't know yet. I need to think a little."

Sophia said, "You know that Silvestri wants the ring. Quite badly."

He nodded. "I just don't see how killing Mariaurora helps him to get it."

"Maybe it just helps to stop our client from getting it."

"Maybe."

It seemed unlikely, but then so did the fact of Mariaurora lying dead on the floor of her subterranean apartment.

He said, "So you know the detective who's investigating?"

"Emiliano?" She nodded. "I was in the police force for a little while, and we've kept in touch." She considered. "He's good at his job." She sipped her drink. "We need to work together, Daniel. You need to be careful, and let me do my job." She looked at him. "This is my city. Only a very arrogant man wouldn't get that. Especially now."

He said, "Thanks for the drink, Sophia."

"You're unbelievable. Where are you going?"

He shrugged. "I think better when I'm moving. See you soon."

He went to the bar to pay, but the barman just smiled and waved him away.

Sophia. Whose city this was. He walked slowly along Via Veneto, away from the grand hotel, following the long curve of the road down to the Piazza Barberini and its great fountain. He sat down on the wall at the water's edge, to review what he knew. The night air was cold, and he thrust his hands into his pockets.

The young man who approached him had a cigarette in his

hand.

"Do you have a light?" he asked.

Daniel shook his head, waiting for him to walk on. The young man, instead, sat down beside him. Daniel looked into speculative blue eyes. It took him a moment to recognise Mario Scipione, less boyish than in his University photograph.

"You're an interesting character, aren't you?" the academic said, in English. Daniel considered him.

"And so, it seems, are you," he said, in Italian.

The other man smiled. "I'm your friend," he said. "I'm quite possibly here to save your life." He found his own lighter, and lit the cigarette. "At this moment, you're safe, because the police are watching you. You did know that, didn't you?" He smiled again. "But that's only for now. And then you won't be safe at all." He took a drag and slowly exhaled smoke. "You're just a mercenary, I get that. So I'm offering you the chance to walk away. Just… walk." He stood up. "Like this." And he smiled and strolled away, nodding towards what Daniel now recognised as an unmarked police car, and disappeared into the shadows of Via Sistina.

The wind gusted again, sharply, and Daniel got to his feet. He perhaps should have expected that Mario Scipione would be here in Rome. He began his walk home, past the Termini terminus, away from the city centre and towards San Giovanni. Rome in the early hours was quiet but not deserted. He passed a couple kissing passionately in a doorway, a pair of slim boys on their rapid way somewhere, huddled figures in sleeping bags on benches. The main traffic at this hour was the occasional white taxi with the city's distinctive red livery. The air was cool and damp, and the moon was surrounded by a pale halo of cloud. He didn't look to see if the police car was still following him. He let himself into his small, silent hotel and quietly took the stairs two at a time to his room. He sat down at the unsteady desk and turned on his laptop.

Chapter Twenty-Four

Dan had never been in a helicopter before. He liked it. There was something very exhilarating about travelling through the skies at noisy speed, and he kept his eyes fixed on the scenery below them. He was quite glad that conversation was impossible.

Eva looked tired, anxious, and somehow still cross with him. This was the Silvestri way of getting them to Milan. They swept northwards, across green countryside and scattered towns, clouds scudding above them, the wind whistling around them, and the helicopter blades clattering.

All too soon, they were coming down to land on a grass rectangle, as neat as a billiard table, at the back of a large office complex built of mirrored blue glass just outside the city. Over its huge doors Dan noticed what he now recognised as the logo of Silvestri Enterprises, which comprised the gothic letters S and E surmounted by a laurel wreath. Back on the ground, his faintly nauseous sense of inadequacy and anxiety began to return. There was a car waiting for them. The driver, in uniform and sunglasses, eased them through the streets of Milan, which were wet with recent rain, and grey with a light, drifting mist. Occasionally, he glanced back at them. The driver had the same look as Piero – neither friendly nor unfriendly, interested or uninterested. Simply professional. It was an unnerving look.

When they arrived at the church which Claudia had described, he got out and opened the doors for them.

"Thank you," Dan said. "Grazie."

The driver inclined his head, and then got back into the car. Eva was looking up at the ancient facade. Dan felt it was a very good sign that the church actually existed, though he didn't say this.

"Shall we?" he asked, and Eva nodded.

They ascended the steps, Dan noticing the ancient stonework, the heavy, weathered doors, the tall, finely-carved stone window frames. Inside, a pervading scent of incense, a radiant Madonna and Child over the altar, and a whole pantheon of saints and bishops silently watching them from the alcoves. He glanced up to see angels and cupids gliding amongst apostles on the ceiling. It was a lovely church. Eva genuflected, having dipped her fingers into a small stone bowl of water and crossed herself. Holy water, Dan realised. Faith was something that always surprised and baffled him.

A large priest, with high colour and slightly laboured breathing, was walking down the aisle towards them. A sudden beam of sunlight struck across the pews, and the priest walked through it, momentarily illuminated. He gravely shook hands with them both, and he and Eva talked in Italian, their voices reverberating in the silence. He nodded from time to time in answer to her questions, and talked at length, occasionally gesturing towards three confessional boxes which stood to one side of an altar where candles were burning. Dan had seen plenty of these in Rome. He understood that the priest would sit on one side, and the person confessing on the other side, and they would communicate through a grille.

He could see that there was a façade around the top of each one, carved with stylised flowers, and presumed that it was in that space that the priest had offered to hide Claudia's case. He was drawn back to the conversation by the change of tone – disappointment in Eva's voice, apology in the priest's. The elderly man then fixed Dan with his pale, bulbous eyes, and attempted an explanation in English, with the air of a swimmer taking on the Channel.

"We didn't know about this," he said. "The priest at that time didn't say anything. Nothing. And he died." He shrugged. "The first we know, a professor comes from the University. He explains us this story, and we let him take a ladder and get up on top of the confessional boxes. We didn't think there would be nothing there. But... He found a case.

A small cardboard one, nearly buried in dust. And he took it away." He sighed. "I didn't think there was anything wrong with this – he was from the University, after all."

"When was this?" Dan asked him.

"Three weeks," the priest replied.

"Three weeks?" Dan repeated. "Wow."

They thanked the priest. Outside, the driver was leaning against the door of the car and smoking a cigarette while he waited, but Eva ignored him and sat down on the church steps. Dan sat down beside her.

"So it was true," she said. "After all those years... I always listened, but I don't think I could ever quite believe what my grandmother told me. I just found it hard to imagine... But it was true." She stood up slowly. "The Father couldn't remember the name of the person from the University," she said. "We don't even know if he really was from there. But... We can go and see what we can find out. Ready?"

Dan nodded, and, below them, the driver swung open the passenger doors.

Chapter Twenty-Five

The blinds were drawn, and in the half-light Daniel could see that the office was still as Francesco Loggi had left it. On the wall behind the desk, a teaching timetable, a poster of the Red Hot Chilli Peppers, several framed Brueghel prints. Bookcases filled two of the other walls, and a filing cabinet stood beside the window, with a sticker of Spiderman on the top drawer. There was a small coffee machine on top of the filing cabinet. Italians didn't do kettles and instant coffee. The desk was orderly – trays for student essays, a stack of printed lecture notes, pens, a couple of photographs in which Francesco smiled from a ski-slope. His computer was gone, no doubt taken by the police, and the room had an air of desolation.

The admin assistant who had let him in shook her head.

"I can't bear to be in here," she said. She was a small, round woman with lustrous black hair curling around her face, and wide brown eyes. "I still can't believe that he isn't coming back." She lowered her voice. "And his research assistant has vanished," she said. "Just... gone. He never seemed like a killer. He was quite sweet."

Daniel blinked. "You think his research assistant killed him?"

She shrugged. "The police didn't hold him, so maybe they think it was someone else," she conceded. "But he found the body. And they were lovers."

"Sabato and Francesco?"

She said curiously, "You know Sabato?"

"Only his name," Daniel said.

She seemed to accept this. "They were in a relationship. It was an open secret. But it seemed to me that Sabato cared more about Francesco than Francesco cared about him.

Well…" She indicated the photographs of Francesco. "He was good looking and also very ambitious, everyone knew that. And gifted. Have you read his books?"

Daniel nodded.

"Of course you have," she said. "Excuse me. You said you knew him through his work."

He nodded again.

"I wonder… Were there any clues in the days leading up to his death? Any phone calls, visitors, people you didn't know…?"

She shook her head. "The police asked me these questions," she said. "I told them – I know he had something on his mind. He was very irritable, and he looked tired. So there was definitely something going on."

"But nothing he talked about? Nothing you heard about?"

She shook her head.

"But he and Sabato quarrelled a lot," she said. "He said once that Sabato was suffocating him."

"You heard this?"

She nodded. "Sabato was trying to get him to go to a wedding he'd been invited to, in the States, but Francesco wouldn't go. He said he couldn't leave Milan." She shrugged. "I don't know what happened in the end. I think Sabato went on his own."

Daniel thanked her. He sat on in the still office. The digital clock on the wall was still marking off the minutes. He had a growing feeling that he understood what had happened to Francesco. He thought again about the academic's notes on the ring of Diocletian, all stored on Dropbox. Sabato had accessed them, and Daniel was sure that others had also been able to. Some of them were cryptic – just initials and abbreviations. Nothing that Daniel could make sense of, but an academic working in the same school, in the same department…? Francesco had been cautious, but not cautious enough.

The admin assistant came back after a few minutes. "I should really lock this room again," she said apologetically.

"Of course." Daniel rose. "Thank you. I appreciate your

help."

Outside, a grey twilight mist had settled on the city, and Daniel walked briskly, heading for the station and his train back to Rome. The Russian called.

"Daniel, we need to talk."

"We're talking."

"Why are you in Milan?"

"I thought I'd take a look at Francesco's office."

"Forget Francesco, Daniel. He didn't find the ring, he just wasted time. Plus he's dead. He's an irrelevance. I'm surprised you don't realise that."

"I'm just trying to be thorough."

"Be thorough in relevant ways, Daniel. And why did your MP call you?"

"What?"

"That call you had. I've had it checked. It was a British MP."

"I don't have an MP."

"Daniel, everyone in the UK has an MP. You can't help it. You think I don't know that? I hope you're not getting confused in your priorities."

Daniel said, "I think that was a crossed line of some sort…" He arrived at Milan's main station, and said, "I'll have to go now, it's too noisy to talk. I'll be in touch." And he switched off the Russian's phone.

On the journey back to Rome, he glanced at a newspaper. Silvestri Enterprises were defending a number of corruption claims, and a photo of Lorenzo Silvestri featured on the business pages, severe as a head teacher, frowning as he swung through a revolving door. Daniel sat back. How rational was it that he was involved in all this? Increasingly, not very. But he was locked into the chase, and too far committed to turn back. He was going to find the ring.

Chapter Twenty-Six

"You hadn't heard?" the professor asked.

She poured tea from a china teapot while she spoke, and offered them digestive biscuits. It was all quite comforting to Dan. Except that there was no milk for the tea. Oh well. He sipped it, added a bit of sugar, sipped again.

"It was terrible. His research assistant found him dead. And the research assistant himself has now disappeared – just vanished – so who knows what has become of him…" The professor shook her head with melancholy relish. She was what Dan imagined a Roman matron would look like – tall, strong-featured, with emphatic eyebrows, only with cropped, dark blue hair, and wearing jeans with her pink silk blouse and voluminous, rose-coloured pashmina.

"There's been lots of speculation, of course," she went on. "It's very scary. The police have been here all the time, interviewing everyone, but I don't think they've got any leads. It's a mystery. I thought it would have been headlines all over Italy, but seemingly not in Rome…"

She helpfully poured more tea into Dan's cup. "But anyway, his field was the later Roman emperors, so this is really rather outside his scope. Mussolini and his aftermath is much more Mario Scipione's specialism." She turned to Dan. "You're not a historian, I gather?"

Dan shook his head apologetically.

"Well, I think Eva would agree with me that the ring is one of those curious artefacts that moves in and out of people's consciousness, and changes its significance with time. Hugely important in the Middle Ages, and in fact right up to the Renaissance, then gradually forgotten; stolen, sold, sold again, and finally claimed by our elected dictator, Mussolini. Your grandmother's story is fascinating, Eva. But as far as I know, no-one in this department is doing any current research..."

She excused herself to answer her phone. Dan and Eva sat in silence until she returned. Dan quietly reasoned that the ring and the death of Francesco Loggi quite probably had nothing whatsoever to do with each other. Coincidences happened all the time...

"Do excuse me," she said. "What were we saying...? Ah yes. Mario Scipione. Now he's someone who's done a lot of work on Mussolini." She lowered her voice confidentially. "Rather right-wing. Regrettable views. But... good family connections. Don't quote me. It might be worth talking to him while you're here. What do you think? Shall I have him over for a cup of tea?" Dan had noticed that most of the professor's questions were, in fact, rhetorical. She was already dialling a number.

"Mario, ciao. Tell me, are you too busy to drop in to my office for ten minutes? I have a couple of friends here..." She beamed. "Excellent." She turned to them. "He's on his way over. It's a fascinating little mystery, isn't it? You never know – he may be able to shed a little light on it. It's a small world, as they say in England..."

A light tap on the door, and they looked up as a fair-haired man, a little less tall and a little more muscled than Dan had somehow imagined, entered the room. He was smiling, his eyes resting on the professor's visitors. He sat down and accepted a cup of tea while the professor made the introductions.

"I taught Eva, a little before your time, Mario... a gifted student. And this is an English visitor, Dan." Dan smiled dutifully, though Mario's gaze didn't really encourage it.

"Fascinating," Mario said, when the professor had finished. "And why, exactly, are you interested in the ring of Diocletian?" His smile was still nominally friendly, but the atmosphere, somehow, wasn't.

Eva said, "My grandmother was curious to know if anyone had found it."

"Really?" Mario said. "And you've come all this way to

try to find out for her? That's very sweet of you."

A definite chill had now entered the room. Mario put his cup down. His eyes flicked contemptuously over Dan, and then he turned to the professor.

"Thanks for the tea. I'm sorry I can't help, but..." He got to his feet. "All sorts of opportunists have tried to appropriate our history," he said coldly to Eva. "It's a pity that your grandmother left the ring where it could be found by someone like that. I hope you have a safe journey back to Rome."

After he had gone, the professor kissed Eva goodbye, and shook Dan's hand.

"I'm sorry Mario couldn't help," she said, "but it was worth a try." She studied Eva's face. "Is everything all right, Eva?" And Eva smiled wanly, and nodded.

It was only after they had left the University, and were being driven back to the big glass building and the helicopter, that she said, "My grandmother could have been mistaken. It mightn't have been anyone from the University who came to see her..."

Dan said, "Could we check with her?"

"We could, but her memory isn't really great. She probably couldn't tell us much about who it was."

Dan, trying not to look smug, produced his phone.

"I took a few shots of Mario," he said. "They're not very good, but they might help."

"Mario? You think...?" Eva's eyebrows had risen.

Dan couldn't have explained why, exactly, but he had a strong feeling about Mario. Something about his eyes, perhaps, or his thin smile. He said, "He just seemed... hostile."

"Well, we can try," Eva said, without much conviction.

Claudia scrutinised the photos with her glasses and a magnifying glass – Mario sipping tea, Mario looking over at the professor, Mario getting to his feet. They were a bit blurred, and she peered at them for some time, while Dan found that he was holding his breath.

Finally she spoke to Eva, who told Dan, "Yes, she thinks

she recognises him." And Dan exhaled with a sense of real achievement.

As they travelled back to Silvestri's villa, Eva said, "But I don't think she was sure."

Silvestri, too, was less than impressed.

"If you're right," he said, "and this is the person who has the ring, then I fail to understand why you're here, and not still in Milan." But even so, he had Dan's photos downloaded, and spoke quietly and at length with Piero. "You will go back to Milan with Piero," he said at last. "We'll investigate this further." To Eva he said graciously, "Please feel free to return to your place of work, signora. And thank you for your assistance."

Dan watched as Eva walked to the car. She looked back at him, and for the first time he saw something like sympathy in her gaze. It was a clear and radiant evening, the sky a gently fading blue, the moon already faintly visible. Dan continued to look out once the limousine had gone. The gardens in this light had the kind of perspective and stillness that he had only seen before in art. There was something almost hallucinatory about their formality. The difference between him and Sam wasn't courage – it was more that Sam would simply not have ended up in this kind of trouble.

Dan wasn't a brave person. He had never pretended to be. He, like most sane human beings, would go quite a long way in order not to have to be brave. But here he was. Waiting for Piero, waiting to go on a journey that could quite feasibly end badly, and with no other choice. Dan watched the shadows deepen and the moon rise.

He wished for the night to be over.

Chapter Twenty-Seven

The sky was black, and thunder occasionally rolled through the city. Torrential rain surged across the pavements, forming fast-moving rivers in the gutters, swirling out into miniature lakes the colour of milky coffee. Daniel was in the vestibule of his hotel. The walls were mirrored, and the desk clerk watched with open curiosity as the detective suggested that they sit down in the two armchairs that filled a gloomy corner next to the lift. He was wrapped in a raincoat, and he slumped in the chair with his hands still in his pockets.

"I know we talked the other evening," he said, "but to be honest, Mr Taylor, you are troubling me just a little." He smiled a small, confiding smile. "Of course this is just to clear things in my mind. It's off the record."

He pulled an electronic cigarette from his pocket, and then put it back again. "Such a stupid habit," he said. "Sophia always tells me to stop." He said this almost absently. "So, Mr Taylor, I understand what you do, and I understand that you are usually successful. But you're not doing very well this time. Is that more or less right?"

Daniel shrugged and nodded slowly.

"You don't like that kind of question," the detective noted. "You possibly think you can still pull it all together. You're used to being on top of things. But here, you're not quite on top."

Daniel said, "Was there something specific I can help you with, Detective…?"

"Yes, actually," the other man said, still slumped, still with his hands in his pockets. "The fact that the family believe you work for an auction house, when in fact you don't, is interesting, but it isn't a breach of the law. The fact that you were first on the scene of a murder is likewise interesting, but not a breach of the law. But the fact that you then went to Milan, to the office of a previous murder victim, makes me curious. Again, it isn't a breach of the law. But you can see, perhaps, that all these non-breaches of the law begin to add up to something that is, well... interesting."

"What has Sophia told you?" Daniel asked.

The detective sighed. "You obviously don't know her. She's completely professional. That's why I'm here, in the rain, in this draughty hallway, having this conversation with you."

Daniel had nothing to lose by talking to the detective. He briefly explained the Francesco Loggi connection, and the detective toyed with the fake cigarette and stared out into the rain and looked tired.

He waited until Daniel had finished, and then said slowly, "You know, Lorenzo Silvestri isn't a man to trifle with, Mr Taylor. He really isn't – ask any Roman." He gestured, incorporating the hallway and the road beyond. "Ask any Italian. He's the reason the Russian has hired Sophia to watch your back." He peered at Daniel. "My advice? My advice to you is to let go of this. Why provoke Silvestri? It's a bloody ring – the Russian can live without it." He shrugged. "But, from what I've heard about you, I'd guess that I'm probably wasting my breath. So let me formally remind you to keep us informed of your whereabouts. We may want to interview you again. Please be available." He stood up. "Thanks for your time."

He fastened the top button on his raincoat and turned the collar up. With a nod to the desk clerk, he walked out into the darkness of the morning and was gone.

Daniel went into the bar next door, dodging the rain, and ordered an espresso. Before the detective's arrival, he had been pondering a phone number he'd noticed amongst Francesco's jottings. It was a Rome code, and Daniel had realised suddenly that he recognised it. He had listened while Livia read it out to Agnese, and Agnese dialled it. It was Mariaurora's number, with a row of fives at the end.

He sat, stirring the coffee, trying to follow this through.

Francesco had called Mariaurora. Had he been stringing the Russian along, having got the ring from Mariaurora, or having possibly duped her, and done a deal elsewhere? A niggling doubt had been troubling him since he arrived, and now, spoon revolving slowly in the small cup, he considered it. It was just possible that Sabato was also in the dark. It was possible that Francesco had been playing a game of his own, and that Sabato, too, had been Scherherazaded. It would mean that this whole trip had been a waste of his time, and the truth lay somewhere else altogether. But... In the meantime he had a meeting with the family. He was just about to leave the bar when Sophia appeared, smiling, big black umbrella dripping in the doorway.

"I missed you at coffee this morning," she said.

Daniel said, more tersely than he had intended, "I've been talking to your friend."

She said, coolly, "I have lots of friends."

"Your friend Emiliano."

"Oh." She nodded. "That friend. Well." She twirled the umbrella. He noticed the faint freckles on her cheekbones, the beads of rain gleaming in her red hair, her grey eyes.

"You'd better let me give you a lift," she said. "It's wet out there." But he was already moving.

"No thanks," he said. "I'm not made of sugar – I won't melt."

She stared at him, and then raised her hands and said to the bar in general, "English. My God. Stubborn." She shouted after him, "Ridiculous!"

He left by one door, and Sophia left by another. Deeply irritated, he made his way to his meeting at Alessandro's villa, where there was something like a council of war.

The key to the safety deposit box, Livia told him, was missing.

"So whoever killed Mariaurora took it," she said. "Maybe that was the reason she was killed. But no-one can open the box without proof of identity, so no-one can open it except one of us. I've talked to the bank. If we can provide a death certificate for Mariaurora..." She paused for a moment, her hand on her throat. "What a thing to have to say. But... If we can, and provide evidence of our identity, and a sworn statement as to what happened to the key, then we can open the box. The problem, Mr Taylor, is that this will all take time."

She and Alessandro exchanged a look.

"That's unless..." she continued carefully. "We talked to a friend at the bank. A family friend. He understands our situation perfectly. And he could help, but unfortunately it would be expensive."

There was a diplomatic silence, and three pairs of blue eyes rested on him.

Daniel said, "Well, it's possible that the collector I mentioned to you, the Russian, would be able to... smooth things, but he'd want to be assured that he was the preferred buyer..."

Three heads nodded. No problem. Daniel called the Russian, and a money transfer was arranged.

"But I'm relying on you to make sure these people are trustworthy, Daniel," the Russian said. "You know how crooked families can be."

And with almost miraculous speed, an appointment was arranged. Early the next morning, Daniel, Livia, Alessandro and Agnese arrived at the discreet, august bank building. The banker who greeted them was bald and bearded, with a friendly smile, and small, surprised-looking eyes behind tortoiseshell glasses. He shook hands, briefly kissed Livia, and then said, "Please. This way."

Cleaners were still polishing the wide mosaic floors, and their footsteps echoed as they were led to a stainless steel lift set into an ancient brick wall, and from there, down several floors to a steel-lined corridor. The banker keyed in a code, followed by a fingerprint and iris scan. Finally, he swiped his security card, and a door slid noiselessly open. They followed him into a vaulted room lined with grey, anonymous boxes, lit by diffuse neon light. It had something of the atmosphere of a catacomb.

"Here is your box," the banker said, indicating one set in

the higher levels of the wall. "It requires both a key and a code for entry," he said, "but there is an over-ride, should the key be lost."

He tapped numbers into the box's small keypad as he spoke, glancing down at a piece of paper.

"This code changes every hour," he said.

No-one was listening to him. All of them were watching as the small, heavy door opened, and the banker drew out an old cardboard box, the shape and size of a shoebox.

"You see?" Livia said. "It's here. It's really here. I told you." She took the box from the banker and opened the lid. Inside was a plain wooden box with a hinged top. Livia lifted it out and handed it to Daniel.

"For your Russian buyer," she said. Everyone was smiling, even the banker.

Daniel opened the box.

Chapter Twenty-Eight

"You're not serious."

"Why would you think we're not serious?"

The three of them were standing in Mario Scipione's office. The young academic's eyes were locked on the imperturbable, enquiring face of Piero.

"Because he's a fool who can't even speak Italian, and your boss is a bigger fool for listening to him." This, anyway, is what Piero translated for Dan. Mario's expression suggested that his actual words were probably more crude than this.

Piero then said, with the slightly weary courtesy that was so intimidating, "I do hope we can have a civilised conversation, Dottore."

Dan wasn't sure how he felt about being on the same side as the man in the green tie. On their long drive to Milan, he had sat in the passenger seat alongside him, and felt like quite a different person to the one who had been driven to Villa Silvestri in the early morning, in what seemed like another lifetime. He was, however, still certain that he was right. Mario knew something.

"And exactly what makes you think that Lorenzo Silvestri has any right to the ring?" Mario now asked.

"That's not really a question we need to consider," Piero said. "In fact, it's irrelevant. Your choices are these, Dottore. Either give the ring to me now, or take me to it, or come with me back to Rome to explain to Signor Silvestri why you are refusing to comply with a simple, and courteous, request."

Mario looked at him for a long moment, and then he smiled.

Piero sighed. "Really, Dottore, you need to make a decision," he said, and produced his gun.

What neither of them had expected was the sudden karate kick which Mario then launched. It knocked down the man in the green tie, and his gun spun out of his hand and fired a shot which crashed thunderously and lodged in the floor. It made only a small, neat hole in one of the tiles, which Dan found surprising in view of the devastating noise. And then Mario walked out, locking the door behind him. Piero got to his feet and dusted down his suit. Then he retrieved his gun.

"Let's go," he said, and imperturbably delivered a kick to the door which caused it to fly open. The small crowd which had gathered outside stood back apprehensively, and Piero walked out with Dan trailing in his wake. No-one tried to stop them.

Back in the limousine, Piero made a brief phone call, and lit a cigarette. He didn't ask Dan if he minded. Luckily Dan didn't.

"I've called Stefan," he said. "Stefan is who we use when civilised means fail. We'll meet him in an hour."

There was, Dan thought, something very Zen-like about Piero. He seemed neither shaken nor upset, whereas Dan's heart was still pounding, his ears ringing, his guts churning. He wasn't at all sure that he wanted to meet a man who was called in when civilised means had failed. He was in the company of scary people, and he wished, with a bitter, futile intensity, that he'd just stayed in Boston with his brother and his family. His parents, even now, were whale-watching and eating clam chowder, and his brother... He suddenly noticed that he had a message from his brother. He had no idea how long it had been there.

How's Rome? the text asked, in Sam's friendly way. Hope the course is going well. Your Italian friend is back with us, staying for a while. Gloria says hello. Talk soon!

Great. Just great. Dan deleted the text with a stab of his finger. Gloria says hello... Your Italian friend is back...

The Italian had been at Sam's wedding. He and Sam had apparently met at a conference, and so there he was, the most beautiful human being that Dan had ever seen. He had been, in the words of an old American show, struck dumb by beauty. He had been unable to do more than gaze, give the odd, wobbly smile when the man met his eyes, and wonder in which of the many multiple, distant universes which simultaneously existed the Italian would conceivably be interested in him, Dan Taylor.

Piero had now thrown his cigarette out of the window and started the car. As they drove, Dan caught a glimpse of a building that rose like a vast ghost, a pale trellis of towers, and he realised that this was the famous cathedral. He craned his neck, but it had gone, and Milan sped past in a blur of rain.

Stefan looked a little more like a stereotypical hardknock than Piero. He had closely-shaven grey hair and intense eyes. He sat back in the restaurant, having ordered mushroom risotto, and scrutinised the photos on Dan's phone. Piero and Dan had both ordered pizza, and the waiter poured all of them glasses of mineral water. Dan had wished for a beer, but had settled for water. When in Milan. They were tucked into a table in the corner, completely screened by the lunchtime crowds, and for the first time Dan saw Piero loosen his tie and sit back. He and Stefan chatted in Italian, and Dan ate, and hoped that the whole thing was now in other hands. Having no Italian, he picked out only occasional words, but recognised "problema" and "università."

After lunch was finished, Piero turned to Dan. "This shouldn't take us long."

And, to his surprise, Dan was deposited at a budget hotel to wait. He thought of escaping. Handing himself in at a police station and asking for help. The man in the green tie had his passport and wallet, but he still had… He still had his phone, and here there was a signal.

Jack. Jack might not be exactly the right person to help him, loud, imperious and impatient as he was, but he was the best that Dan could do. And if necessary, he could talk to the Home Secretary, and insist that Dan be brought home at once. He called.

"Jack, I've got a problem…"

"So finally you've found your phone and you suddenly

remember who I am," Jack said. "Well, let me tell you that your job is going to be in this week's press, and your things from the office are in a box in the nearest Oxfam shop. Oh – and I've found Mrs Morris's file. Goodbye, Dan."

"Jack, wait..." But he had gone.

"You can't just sack me while I'm on holiday," he texted.

"Yes I can," came the reply. "And I have."

"I'm in trouble," he texted.

"That's right," Jack texted back.

Chapter Twenty-Nine

The family had been disbelieving at first.

"Of course it's the ring," Alessandro said, impatiently. "Look at it. Just look at it, Daniel."

Daniel sensed that Alessandro, and possibly Livia, now suspected that he was trying to trick them. There it was: a thick band of dark metal, and a wide flat stone of red and white stripes. He picked it up and handed it to Alessandro.

"Feel it," he said. Alessandro weighed it in his hand.

"I don't understand," he said, as it bounced easily in his palm. Livia silently took it from him and made the same gesture. Something had come back to Daniel from what Sabato had told him.

"The ring was actually too heavy for Mussolini," he said. "He had a copy made, which he wore, and he kept the original for sealing documents. Somehow, you've ended up with the copy."

"But Mariaurora was killed," Livia said. "Surely not just for a copy…"

"I'm sorry," Daniel said. It seemed a bit inadequate.

"We need to know how this has happened," Alessandro said. "We need to know where the original is. It's our property. Our inheritance." His colour had risen. "Someone has stolen it from us," he said, throwing the ring back into the box contemptuously. "We need to know who. Maybe we already know." He seemed rather more upset about this than he had been over the death of his sister. "This cannot stand," he said. "It will not stand."

Livia was just shaking her head. "I don't understand," she said. "If this is a copy, where is the real ring? What happened to it?" She reached out a distressed hand to Agnese, who took and patted it. "Poor, poor Mariaurora…" she said.

The banker slowly herded them out of the vault, and the doors closed behind them. In the breezy morning, Livia said, "We've wasted your time, Daniel. So sorry."

Daniel said, "No, not at all. I'm sorry it's such a disappointment." And he meant it.

Alessandro took his hand in a large handshake, and Agnese embraced him, her lips soft as she kissed his cheek. Livia, too, kissed him, her eyes brimming.

And that had been the last he had seen of them – a small, bereft group outside the doors of the bank, Agnese with her arm around Livia.

His next day started badly. He slept late, after being awake until dawn, and felt groggy as he showered and dressed and made his way to the bar for coffee. No Sophia. He took a seat outside, along with the smokers huddled in the early morning chill, ordered cappuccino and orange juice, and shook his head to try to clear it.

It occurred to him that he still hadn't heard anything from Julian. He called his number, but the call went straight through to voicemail. Should he be worried? It was extremely unlikely, but… He texted him. Julian, call me.

He took a sip of orange juice and picked up a free local paper which someone had left behind on a nearby table. Three young women at the next table were eating cornetti, and chatting. A gloomy middle-aged man brought his coffee out and sat down at the same table as Daniel, but on the other side, and opened his own newspaper. The waiter came round to collect cups and glasses, empty ashtrays, wipe tables. The sky was grey, but the sun was beginning to shimmer behind it, and there was the promise of a bright day.

As the first rays of sunshine lit the pavement in front of the bar, and the scent of cigar smoke drifted past him, the young women rose, the waiter lifted their empty cups from the table, and the man opposite to him shook out his paper and turned the page. Daniel would remember every detail of this moment.

A couple passed by, laughing. And then he seemed to both hear and feel a short series of explosions, while being flung to the ground by the force of another body. Tables fell, people screamed, a pigeon flew across the cobbles, Daniel's face was on the ground, close to a crushed cigarette end, and, as he tried to move, he became slowly aware of a pain in his left leg. He made another effort, and the weight which had been on top of him lessened, and he found himself looking up into the wide, shocked eyes of Sophia.

"Daniel, wait, stay still…" She was on her phone. "Yes, an ambulance. A man has been shot…" Daniel said something, or thought he did, and felt the pain becoming an intense pulse that rocked him with its force. He was aware of warm wetness, and then of Sophia pulling off her scarf and tying it tight around his calf. After that, he remembered very little except pain and darkness.

Chapter Thirty

Dan was still in the hotel when they returned. He'd sat in the guest lounge for over an hour. American and German visitors had passed him by on their way to their rooms, or on their way out with maps and backpacks.

In theory, he could have approached them, any of them, and said, I'm a British citizen and I'm being held by a ruthless Italian industrialist who has got my passport... Please help me.

But he didn't do this, even though he knew he should at least try. It wasn't just that he doubted he'd be believed. Something else, he realised, was now in play. He had somehow become interested in how all this turned out. He had experienced an instinctive and powerful dislike of Mario Scipione, which led him to half hope that Piero and Stefan would return with him in the back of the limousine. Stockholm syndrome. He was identifying with his captors. This didn't make him feel any better about himself.

He sank into a gloomy apathy, not helped by the mustard upholstery all around him and the green, grass-like floor tiles. This was an unusually horrible hotel. He eyed the bar, but it was closed. He got another message from Sam. It seems like things have been happening in Rome – tell you all about it when we talk! He didn't bother to reply.

He could picture Sam as he relaxed in his spacious New England home, chatting with the Italian, cheerfully interested, as he always was, while his glamorous wife poured them drinks and smiled. Life had been a carpet for Sam, right from when he was a bright four-year-old. He'd sailed through everything. Even so, Dan had worked hard at being pleased for him and proud of him in line with the family consensus. But there had been cracks. He had attended the party his parents had thrown to celebrate Sam's first doctorate, and then realised that Sam was actually going on somewhere else to celebrate with his university friends, leaving the family, including Dan, to the leftover champagne and dips. His parents weren't seemingly offended by this, but Dan had been deeply and irrationally angered. He nursed grudges against Sam with a vengeful relish which even he knew was a bit odd. Sam, after all, had always been a good brother in his own way, genuinely pleased by Dan's few moments of success. Dan had been particularly annoyed that Sam had been so positive about him being gay.

He switched his phone off irritably.

Finally the limousine glided back into the hotel's forecourt. Piero actually gave him a smile – a wry, defeated smile – as he came into the lounge. Stefan sighed and eased himself onto a bar stool, and a hotel employee immediately came over and switched the lights on. So that was how you opened the bar.

"Apparently he took a flight to Rome yesterday," Piero said, ordering a fruit juice. "Not long after our conversation with him, in fact." Stefan ordered a mineral water.

Dan wanted to conform, but his need for alcohol was too great, and he ordered a glass of red wine. A small bowl of crisps, and another of nuts, appeared alongside his glass. This always seemed to happen in Italy – why didn't it happen in the UK? He munched, and drank, and listened. Piero glanced at his watch and yawned.

"If we leave now, we'll be back for around midnight. We can pick him up tomorrow."

His certainty was chilling. Outside, he lit a cigarette, and he and Stefan tossed a coin for who should drive. Dan thought, very briefly, of making a stand even now. He could refuse to get into the car. He could run back into the hotel, shouting for help. He could demand protection from these thuggish characters.

But he didn't. He got into the back seat of the limousine, and, before long, with the dark road flashing past him, he was asleep.

Chapter Thirty-One

"Really, Daniel, you do get yourself into trouble…"

The voice slowly found its way through his troubled, drugged dreams, and Daniel smiled, and opened his eyes. Julian peered down at him, his expression a mix of concern, reproach, and surprise. He was dressed in the clerical black that he always wore, and Daniel found it, and his presence, deeply reassuring.

"I'm in hospital?" he hazarded. His voice came out as a croak.

"You are. A rather expensive one," Julian said cheerfully.

Daniel slowly raised his head. He was in a small white room, inhaling a smell made up of soap powder, disinfectant, and a fainter scent of mimosa that came from the vase of dazzling yellow beside the bed.

"You've been shot," Julian added, in his practical way. "Luckily, the bullet lodged in your calf, and they've been able to remove it without it doing any permanent damage. You'll be good as new, apparently."

Daniel managed a smile. "And I was concerned about you," he said.

"Well, I did have a rather odd visit to Lorenzo Silvestri's place," Julian said. "He seemed to have got you confused with a tourist, and I never did get to the bottom of why he'd invited you to dinner anyway… You're not a friend of his, are you?"

Daniel shook his head.

"Glad to hear it."

Daniel laid his head down again. "Sophia was there."

"She saved your life," Julian said. "She threw herself at you and knocked you over, so only one of the bullets hit you, and it hit your leg, and not your thick head. She also stopped you bleeding to death. Remarkable young woman." He eyed his brother. "You look like you could do with a little more rest," he said. "I'll go now. I'll be back tomorrow."

Daniel nodded, or thought he did. And then it was evening, and he was fully awake, and in pain. His leg was tightly bandaged, so he couldn't see the wound. He slept again.

The next morning he took his first cautious steps out of bed, supported by a crutch and a nurse, and was sitting in a chair next to the window when the detective strolled into the room. Daniel watched him perch himself on the edge of the bed.

"Interesting development," he said, glancing at Daniel's chart. "I won't say I told you so. Any thoughts?"

Daniel shook his head. "Did anyone see the gunman?"

"Yes, several people," the detective answered. "But the descriptions aren't great. He was crouching behind a parked car, wearing a hood and with a scarf up over his face. He fired three times, and then ran." He sniffed the mimosa. "We're checking the bullets we've recovered, and it's possible that they're from the same gun that killed the woman you found. So..." He glanced at Daniel's leg. "I think on the whole you've been lucky. Our enquiries are continuing. We'll take a full statement from you later today. Your doctor thinks you'll be up to it – she says you're making a pretty good recovery. Meanwhile, I take it you didn't see anything?" He looked unsurprised when Daniel shook his head. "Apparently you were reading a paper," he said. "Well, we'll be in touch." He rose. "And we'll have someone keeping an eye on you here."

And he went, quietly closing the door behind him.

Outside the window, the sky was flickering between light and cloud, and Daniel watched while the sun was gradually extinguished. He called Sabato and got his voicemail.

"Sabato, call me. It's urgent," he said irritably. It was clear enough now that Sabato had been right to flee Italy – the only question was whether he'd fled far enough.

Then came a call from the Russian.

"What is going on over there, Daniel? Did you see who shot you?"

"No, but I'm pretty sure I know who it was," he said. "The police are investigating."

"The police," the Russian said contemptuously. "They'll find nothing. You know who is behind this, Daniel?"

"Yes, probably..."

"There's no probably about this. This is Lorenzo Silvestri's signature. It's obvious. He's a detestable, shameless creature, greedy beyond all human belief, who thinks he can intimidate the world. I've had dealings with him, and you can believe me. But if he thinks he can get away with shooting my trusted agent – and you are my trusted agent, Daniel – then he will soon learn. Very soon. I've taken steps, which you don't need to know about. And meanwhile, please co-operate with Sophia."

Daniel said, "This wasn't Silvestri. It was someone else..."

The Russian said, "No, you're wrong, Daniel. You should have listened to me and to Sophia. You know she's ex-army? No?" A brief, perplexed pause. "I don't know what you've been doing over there, Daniel. You don't seem to know very much. You seem to be misinformed. I need better reports from you, Daniel. If I had better reports, I wouldn't need to keep ringing you. I'm concerned. Can you walk?"

Daniel managed to end the conversation, on the understanding that they'd talk again tomorrow.

And then there was a commotion outside the door, raised voices, and three people burst in: Alessandro, Agnese and Livia, the latter almost hidden behind a vast bunch of tiny yellow flowers.

"Daniel, how dreadful," she said, dumping the bouquet on his bedside table, and embracing him. "Oh good – you already have mimosa," she added, with an approving nod at his vase. "Today is the eighth of March – we celebrate the end of winter, and men buy mimosa for women. Or vice versa sometimes. It's a very nice tradition." She sat down in a chair opposite to him. "Dear Daniel, we're so sorry." She glanced at Alessandro, who nodded.

"It's shocking," he said. "Very." He also took a seat, while Agnese found a vase for the flowers.

"We want you to come and recuperate with us," Livia said. "In fact, we won't take no for an answer." She held up an imperious hand to silence Daniel. "I know Alessandro's place is very horrible," she said, "but it's also out of the way, and the one thing it has got is space. There's a guest suite upstairs where you'd be perfectly comfortable, and there would be peace and quiet. What else do you need?" Again, a raised hand cut off his answer. "This is at least partly our fault – or at least the fault of our wretched family – and you must give us the opportunity to make amends, just a little."

Daniel was in the midst of thinking up a convincing reason why it would be better for him to just book into a hotel for a few days, when Julian arrived. After a lot of handshakes, Livia explained their plan. Julian looked pleased.

"That's very, very kind," he said. "It's the perfect solution. And of course he's going to need a little looking after, until he's well enough to fly home." And he shot a reproachful look at his younger brother.

Daniel had been twelve years old, a quiet, bright boy, when he'd been involved in the accident. His father had been driving, with his mother in the passenger seat, and he had been in the back of the car. It had been a head-on collision at night with an old van which was on the wrong side of an unlit country road. The other driver, who had also died, had been seventeen years old, and on his way to see his girlfriend. The vehicles had both been reduced to twisted, smoking metal. Daniel didn't remember a great deal about the crash itself, but he'd been in hospital for a long time afterwards, and those weeks had made an indelible mark on him. He remembered the nights, listening to the sounds of the ward, looking at the light at the nurses' station, waiting for his injuries to heal. He had had time to absorb the devastating unreliability of life. Sometimes in his sleep he still heard the voices of the firefighters who had cut him loose. This one's alive, one of them had said.

Daniel had learnt then that there wasn't any recovery from loss. It had just become part of who he was. It had grown with him, like the long, thin scar that ran from his ribs to his hip. The world, it seemed to him now, had somehow lost its colour at the moment of the collision, and it had only ever come back in darker tones. Even the sunshine of Italy had never dazzled him. He had managed since then as best he could – he used his intelligence. He created answers.

Julian had already been twenty-one, and studying at a seminary in Rome. They had very little family, and so it was agreed that Daniel would attend boarding school in England during term time, and come over to Rome during the holidays. He had spent long Christmas, Easter and summer vacations at various language schools in the city, accommodated with other foreign students. They generally stayed for a week or a month, whereas in the summer he was there for seven weeks. He learnt Italian, listlessly familiar with every book and every audio tape used by every school. He wandered, creating his own mental maps of Rome, and he consumed Italian thrillers and horror novels. And he remembered the joy and astonishment he had felt when he had seen, for the first time, a noisy flock of green parrots high up in the trees in the gardens at Villa Borghese. It had struck him that birds were always provisional, always temporary, and yet dazzlingly vivid and present. It had been a sudden flash of colour, an inexplicable consolation. And occasionally it still was.

On Thursdays Julian had a free day, and they would go out, travelling as far as the beautiful water gardens at the Villa d'Este at Tivoli, or the coast. On Sundays Daniel would go to the seminary's communal lunch, and then in the afternoon he and Julian would play chess. They were quite evenly matched, and their games went on sometimes over weeks; long, complex wars of attrition. Daniel remembered them as the happiest times of his life in Rome. Why hadn't Julian come back to England? It didn't seem to have occurred to anyone that he should, and the question had crossed Daniel's mind only as an adult. It had been a curious upbringing. He hadn't been actively unhappy, or at least not as far as he remembered. He'd become resigned to regimented living and tedium. He'd excelled both academically and at sports, and had simply waited until he was old enough to move on to university and begin his own life.

It was a life which he had always lived on his own terms. Now, however, he was suddenly surrounded by people, all of whom had strong opinions as to what he should do next.

Agnese turned her serious eyes on him.

"Say yes," she said.

Chapter Thirty-Two

Gunfire crashed through his dreams, and then suddenly he was awake and being dragged from the limousine, and Stefan was kneeling behind the open driver's door, returning fire with a large handgun. He was shooting at a car which had pulled off the road two hundred metres ahead of them, and was facing them, its headlights streaming in the darkness. The limousine was also off the road, one of its lights shot out.

"Who are these people?" Piero asked him tersely, as they crouched behind Stefan.

Dan shook his head. "I have no idea."

Piero muttered something. Stefan paused to reload. Up to now, Dan had only seen him eating and drinking and chatting. Now, he looked like a man doing his job. He coolly took aim again, while bullets from the other vehicle continued to fly around them. Several more carefully-placed shots from Stefan, and then silence.

"Bingo," Piero said approvingly, and they both strolled away from Dan and towards the other car.

In the light of their remaining headlight, Dan could just make out a limp arm dangling from the passenger side of the vehicle they were approaching. He realised that every muscle in his body was clenched and he couldn't move. He could barely breathe.

Let this be a dream. Let this be something I wake up from.

But the sour taste of the night air, the intensity of the lights from both vehicles, the dents in the limousine's bullet-proof body, the silent trees beyond the road, all told him that he was already awake.

With an effort, he straightened out of his crouch, let go of the edge of the car door, pulled himself upright. He realised that he had begun to shake – not violently, but quietly, and all over. This was probably called trembling. He watched Piero and Stefan walk back from the other car, as vividly illuminated as actors on a stage. Their faces were stern. As he watched, smoke began to billow from the other car, followed by flames.

Jesus, Dan thought. Jesus. They've set it on fire.

"Look at what we found," Piero said, as he and Stefan opened the doors of the limousine. He held up a mobile phone, on which there were pictures of Dan, Piero and Stefan, obviously taken hastily as they got into the car, together with a photo of their registration number. There was also a Russian passport. Piero took Dan by the elbow and steered him back into the car.

"You've got some explaining to do, my friend," he said, while Stefan gunned the engine and the limousine glided back onto the road.

Behind them, the other car burned.

Chapter Thirty-Three

Livia was at Alessandro's front door to welcome him. And there, serene as always, was Sophia.

"Hello, Daniel."

"Hello, Sophia." He paused and shifted on his crutch. "I don't think I've said thank you for saving my life."

"Well, someone had to." For the first time, they smiled at each other.

"You didn't tell us you had a colleague," Livia said. "We're putting her up in the lodge in the gardens."

"I'm sure that's not necessary..." Daniel said, but Livia shook her head.

"It's no problem, I promise. It's a pleasure. We want you to have everything you need. We want you to get better and then find the ring. The real ring." And with her agenda set out, she helped Daniel up the stairs.

The guest suite was on the first floor. It was large, with a faint smell of damp, and a haphazard mix of furniture that ranged from nineteenth-century rosewood to 1960s plastic. Livia showed him the bedroom, which contained a spacious but lumpy four-poster bed, and a view over the desolate back gardens, where a long-abandoned hot-tub was covered with dead leaves and bird droppings.

"We usually take lunch at around two. Will that be okay for you?"

This was fine for him. There was phone reception here, and (Alessandro had assured him) wi-fi.

"The bell is there, on the wall, and we will hear it downstairs and bring you anything you need. So just put your leg up and concentrate on getting well." Livia, with majestic kindness, gestured towards the bookcase. It contained paperbacks including Dennis Wheatley novels, The Valley of the Dolls, and numerous biographies of 1960s boxers, racing drivers, and film stars. "Plenty to read," she added, and then blew him a kiss and left the room.

Daniel listened to her footsteps receding down the staircase. He set up his computer, and then edged into the bathroom to take a cautious shower, keeping his bandaged leg dry. While he stood under the old, powerful showerhead and turned his face up to the water, there was a discreet cough, and he turned to see Agnese, holding a set of sheets, studying him with a smile.

"A little on the skinny side," she noted. He abruptly snapped a towel around his waist. Agnese sat down on the bed, apparently oblivious to having embarrassed him.

"I'm sorry about all… this," she said, waving a hand around the room, in an echo of her aunt's gesture.

"It's fine," Daniel said, hobbling back into the bedroom, conscious of the pale scar that ran down his side. He added, "It's kind of your family."

Agnese sighed. "You didn't know them in their heyday," she said. "I didn't either, of course. But they really were something. Have you seen any of my dad's films? No? They're dreadful, really, mostly soft porn, but he was so popular. So handsome. And Livia too – so gorgeous… They were lions. Italian lions in California. But it just faded out. They never had any sense with money, and it all seeped away." She sighed again. "And I can't stay here forever. I need to get back home." She smiled at him. "They've put a lot of hope into this ring thing," she said. "And they like you. So… this is the least we can do. Lunch in half an hour." And she stood up, and was gone.

Daniel felt a low, intense pain in his leg. He pulled his clothes on. His instinct was to lie down, but he resisted it. He set up his computer. He needed to get back on track.

Lunch was served by Livia, who was wearing a quilted waistcoat and a bright turquoise scarf. They ate slightly scorched risotto and fish. Afterwards, he declined a brandy with Alessandro, and hobbled slowly back up to his room. He had just settled down at his desk when there was a tap at the door, and he opened it to Sophia.

"I've found some decent coffee," she said. "There's a bar at the end of the road." She handed him a small cardboard cup with a lid, and then scattered a packet of sugar into her own cup and stirred it. "It's pretty cold in here," she said, wrapping her coat more tightly around herself. "But it's also pretty secluded, so hopefully you'll be safe here for a little while." She sipped her coffee.

"I didn't know you'd been in the army," he said.

She nodded. "Before the police," she said. "I didn't last very long there, either. I'm just not very good at taking orders." She smiled. "So now I do basically what I want. Rather like you." She glanced at his computer. "You're keeping on trying, then."

He nodded.

"Good," she said. "I think I'm beginning to quite like stubbornness. Very British." She smiled her good-humoured smile.

After she had gone, leaving the faintest trace of perfume behind her, Daniel turned back to his work and concentrated on putting her out of his mind.

Chapter Thirty-Four

"Why did the Russian attack the car?"

"I don't know."

"I've been very patient with you up to now, Mr Taylor."

"I don't know. I don't know anything. I... really don't."

He was on a chair in Lorenzo Silvestri's boardroom. Silvestri was at the top of the glass table, flicking through a pile of paperwork as though Dan had stopped being of any interest to him at all. Dan was at the bottom of the table, and Piero and Stefan were sitting on either side of him. Piero was leaning back, Stefan leaning forward, and both were looking at him with very mild curiosity.

"If I was really working for this Russian," Dan said with sudden conviction, "why would he want to kill me?"

"I don't know," Silvestri said, adjusting his glasses and looking up at Dan. "You tell me."

"I don't know. I'm here on holiday to study Roman art." This now sounded so unlikely to his own ears that he could feel the last word trailing away.

The billionaire neatly squared the papers on the polished desk, and glanced over at Piero. "What do you think?"

Piero shrugged. "The Russian usually employs competent people," he said. "This one..." He shrugged again, and glanced at Stefan, who also shrugged.

Silvestri considered this, and slowly and thoughtfully nodded agreement. "But... Mr Taylor was very sure about Mario Scipione."

It was Piero's turn to nod. "He was." And they both looked enquiringly at Dan.

"I... was just trying to... Well, yes. I was sure. Fairly sure. He's... There's something about him..." Dan's mouth began to dry. How had his life ended up like this? Piero now leaned forward slightly, and Stefan leaned back. Dan made a conscious effort not to flinch. He swallowed hard.

"Well, we'll talk to him, and then we can take a view," Silvestri said, after pausing for a moment to see if he was going to start making sense, and clearly deciding that he wasn't. "If it turns out that you're right, Mr Taylor, then you will have assisted us, and that will be the end of the matter. If, however, it turns out that you're wrong, well, we may see this as one more attempt at dissembling and deceit. These are qualities we punish." The hard little eyes rested on him. "You will remain my guest until we've established the truth of the situation." He glanced from Piero to Stefan. "I'll wait to hear from you."

As they got to their feet, Silvestri said, "Just for information, Mr Taylor – what happened to my car last night was provocative in the extreme. I don't tolerate such behaviour, as your employer will soon learn. He has made a most serious misjudgement."

"I don't…"

"All right. Basta." He held up a hand. "It's just possible that you really are the fool you appear. We will see. Now, please return to the morning room." He picked up his large, black desk phone. The interview was over.

Dan walked back slowly between Piero and Stefan. Neither of them looked at him. They opened the doors, and, once he had stepped inside the room, closed them again. He heard the key turn in the lock. Was this really how he was going to die? He could envisage the gun in Stefan's casual hand, his body being tossed from a moving car, Silvestri's cold, indifferent blink. He watched through the windows as Piero and Stefan made their purposeful, unhurried way from the house towards the car. He tried to stop shaking.

Chapter Thirty-Five

The detective had arrived in the late afternoon, and eased himself into an elderly bath-chair in Daniel's room. He glanced around.

"Sophia said it was cold in here." he said. "But I suppose if you're British you don't notice." He carefully rewound his scarf. "It's the damp," he said. "Old places like this, even here in Rome…"

Daniel said, "How can I help you, Detective?"

"Well, we have a situation," the other man said, and Daniel noticed the dark circles under his eyes. "There was an incident last night outside the city. A hire car was shot up and set on fire, and we found a dead Russian inside it. His passport was missing, but we've managed to name him today. We think he worked for your client." He studied Daniel. "What do you think?"

Daniel felt the room's cold creeping into his spine. He nodded slowly.

"It's possible. He could have sent someone. He's angry that I got shot. He thinks Silvestri is responsible."

"Is that what you think?"

"No. It isn't."

"We've spoken to Silvestri, but he's got nothing to say to us, either about your shooting or the incident last night. And the Russian won't speak to us at all. These two are giants, Mr Taylor. If they decide to fight, we're all likely to get hurt."

Daniel said, "I can try to talk to the Russian again."

The detective nodded slowly. "Do that," he said. "We really don't want this to escalate." His eyes didn't leave Daniel. "And I'm seriously considering taking you in to protective custody. I don't think you're helping this situation."

Alessandro had entered the room in time to hear this.

"Nonsense," he said. "Daniel has been injured while trying to help my family. Is that a crime? Of course it isn't. He's a guest in this country and in this house."

"I'm just thinking of his safety," the detective said shortly. "And everyone else's."

"I can protect my house," Alessandro said.

"I don't intend it to come to that," the detective answered. "Sophia's good, but she isn't Sylvester Stallone." He hesitated. "Okay. For now, we'll allocate a guard here. And we'll see how things develop." He stood up slowly. "And let me know when you've spoken to your client, Mr Taylor."

And he left, his footsteps sounding on the old wooden boards.

The Russian was irritated by his call. "I know my own business best, Daniel," he boomed. "You should be concentrating on your business. What progress is there on the ring? Huh? The answer is none. No progress. Silvestri is pissing all over us. The man is a murdering sociopath. Do you know what a sociopath is, Daniel? It's a person like Silvestri." His voice rose. "I need you doing your job, finding the ring, getting out of Rome. None of this is good. You think I haven't got other things to think about? You think I'm not busy? You're starting to be a disappointment to me, Daniel. A big disappointment."

Daniel tested his leg, and decided that, with his crutch, he could walk well enough. He had made a decision which scared him. Up to now, it hadn't really mattered that the Russian was crazy. But now... The pain in his leg echoed his grinding frustration. He was close, he knew it.

He went again over the pieces of information that he had gathered, and mapped out the possibilities. The deaths of Francesco and Mariaurora, and the attempt on his life, all had a single focus behind them. The killer was looking for the ring and hadn't yet found it. Francesco's notes had included the names of staff at Mussolini's Rome palazzo, Villa Torlonia, and a few contact numbers.

He had called them, mainly drawing a blank. An elderly

lady crossly said that she was tired of answering questions, and wasn't going to answer any more. She wanted some peace, which was not much to ask after all these years. No-one had cared about Il Duce all this time. No-one cared about the disgrace of his betrayal and his death, when he was one of the greatest heroes Italy had ever known. And then suddenly there had been phone calls, and visits, and even her grand-daughter had been caught up in it all. Had even gone to the church in Milan. Had even spoken to the priest. If they couldn't respect the dead, so many years later, surely the least they could do was leave them in peace. But if Lorenzo Silvestri was involved, there would be no respect. His family had profited from the war, had kept on profiting ever since... Daniel had thanked her and apologised for disturbing her.

So someone had found the ring, in the dust of the church in Milan.

He looked again at the photograph of Mario Scipione, the man who had warned him at the fountain. A right-winger, a martial arts expert, an erstwhile member of the group which had placed a guard of honour around Mussolini's grave. But rational enough to be a sharp and able academic. He glanced over the articles and lectures that remained online – Scipione had toned down his rhetoric since taking up his post at the University. Of course Daniel had no evidence, nothing to give to the detective, nothing to convince the Russian. All he had was an instinct that recognised Scipione's hunger.

In his two days in the villa, he had become used to being public property. Livia sailed serenely in and out of his room, Agnese popped her head round the door, Alessandro dropped in to chat. It was both intrusive and comforting. They had found him an elderly electric heater which Alessandro plugged cautiously into the wall. It sparked and gave off smoke as the dust which had settled on the bars burned.

"That's better," Livia said. "More like home." She looked at him. "You don't have a wife?" she asked.

He shook his head.

"Or a pretty girlfriend to look after you?"

Again, he shook his head.

She tutted disapprovingly. "No wonder you're thin."

He had ordered the taxi for eleven in the evening. He sat through dinner while Alessandro talked. His topics were the disgraceful behaviour of Lorenzo Silvestri, one of whose companies owned the mortgage on the villa, and was threatening to foreclose.

"This country," he said bitterly. "We allow scum to rise, and he is the result. His family was fascist when it suited the times, then anti-fascist. All the time criminals. All the time making money. And our family..." He made a broad, eloquent gesture of disgust. "I should have stayed in California," he confided, as Livia and Agnese cleared the table. "I should have stayed with Agnese's mother. Or her sister." He lapsed into gloomy silence. "But I know where the ring is, Daniel," he said. "That's what I meant to tell you. We'll talk later."

Sophia had excused herself from dinner. She was probably with Emiliano, Daniel thought. He shut out that image. Agnese, having helped with the dishes, drifted off to her room, and Livia kissed him goodnight and retired for her evening bath. Alessandro remained at the table, bleary-eyed, glass in hand.

"I've figured it out," he told Daniel. "We just need to agree a plan, you and I. I'll come up to you later on."

Daniel had therefore eased himself carefully down the stairs when his taxi arrived, and moved as quietly down the hall as his crutch would allow. He still wasn't certain what he was going to either do or say. He sat back and watched as the car picked up speed along the road into the city, buildings and trees sliding past. He could see his face reflected in the window – thin, sharp features, cool eyes. His phone rang, but he didn't look at it. It didn't matter who it was.

And then they had arrived. The pine trees of Rome hovered overhead, distinctive as sculptures, and above them the moonlit clouds were unmoving. He paid the driver, hauled himself out of the cab, and limped across the park that overlooked the Colosseum, to a bench where a figure sat waiting for him.

Chapter Thirty-Six

Dan had spent the day pacing the spacious room, from window to door and wall to wall. A young man, presumably a guard, had brought him water, and later a lunch of bread and cheese, which he hadn't touched. He was trapped, a wasp in a jar, buzzing helplessly. The daylight in the room had gradually faded. There was a light switch on the wall, but he hadn't pressed it. He had preferred the gathering darkness.

It still seemed to him as though he'd stepped into some kind of strange alternative universe. According to Ellie, Silvestri was globally important, someone whose views were of interest to the stock markets of London, New York, Tokyo. How could such a person also be a criminal? How could he live in a magnificent palazzo, and head a huge international company – and at the same time be responsible for what was apparently gang warfare?

Dan had already witnessed a death, a crime, and Stefan and Piero seemed more than capable of calmly carrying out more crimes. His death would be one of them. He sank onto a chair, overwhelmed by the realisation that he wasn't going to get out of this room alive. These were his last hours. He could hear his own breathing as he never had before, and feel his heart beating. He felt unbelievably alive. He began to pray, although he had no God to pray to.

And then the door opened, and he leapt to his feet, the chair falling over behind him. It took him a panicked moment, in the darkness, to see that it was the interpreter who had entered the room.

Facing him unerringly, she said, "Mr Taylor. Mr Silvestri says that you are free to go."

"What?"

"You may leave whenever you wish."

"I can go?"

"Yes." There was no trace of a smile, but again he thought that he sensed a slight sympathy. She held the door of the morning-room open, and led him along a corridor to the lit, echoing entrance hall. For the first time, Dan saw the lifesize Roman statues, the vast, gilt-framed battle scenes. A servant in black swung open the enormous front door.

"Goodbye, Mr Taylor," the interpreter said, and handed him his passport.

Chapter Thirty-Seven

Mario watched him as he approached. Daniel was aware of the main road below them, still busy, and the dark light of the Colosseum beyond. Was this a public enough place for him to be safe? It was unlikely. There were black, silent trees around them. It would only take a fascist with a rifle to his shoulder, waiting for Mario's slow nod...

He sat down, a little distance from the other man, and laid his crutch between them.

"So you're still here," Mario said.

"And you too," Daniel said. "Aren't your students missing you?"

"You haven't found the ring," Mario said.

"No," Daniel said. "And neither have you."

"No."

A sudden soft scurry, and a rat ran across the path and disappeared.

Mario said, "So, what did you have in mind, Mr Taylor?"

"I thought it might be useful for us to talk."

The other man smiled slowly. "Why would I talk to you?"

"It might help."

"If you knew anything, you wouldn't be here."

"I'm here because I don't want to be shot again."

A gamble. A silence. An owl cried from somewhere nearby.

"Then talk," Mario said.

"You think Francesco found the ring."

Mario laughed softly. "Found the ring, Mr Taylor? Found the ring? He stole it. He stole it from me." He gazed at Daniel. "You didn't know that? I was the one. I'd been looking for it since I was a teenager – ever since I read about it. I wanted it for Mussolini's grave. Just like the old woman in Rome did. But not for it to be buried with him. No. I wanted it to be there on display, as a symbol of our strength and continuity."

He paused and lit a cigarette.

"This wasn't his field – he had no fucking idea what he was doing. So he got into my computer, into my notes, and he copied everything, thieving little prick. And then he went to the church and he stole it."

"But he didn't have it when he died."

"No," Mario said. "He didn't."

"So he had done... What? Sold it on? Mailed it to a friend...?"

Mario said, "I don't think so. He didn't have time."

"And you didn't have time to ask him."

"No."

"Inconvenient."

Mario inclined his head. There was a silence.

"Sabato?" Mario asked.

"He was in the States," Daniel said. "He didn't get back until after Francesco was dead."

Mario shrugged sceptically. "So your ideas are...?"

Daniel shook his head. "We don't actually know for certain that the ring was in Milan. We only have the word of one elderly woman. There were other possibilities, and other people to ask. Mariaurora was one. Unfortunately she died as well." He stretched out his leg carefully to ease it. "You work with some difficult people, Mario."

Mario shrugged. "We do what we have to."

Daniel raised an eyebrow. "Killing the people who might know where the ring is isn't a great strategy."

Mario smiled again.

"Our strategy is to make sure that everyone understands that it is ours. Not the Russian's, not Silvestri's, but Italy's."

He lit another cigarette, the flame briefly reflected in his eyes.

"You think I have a problem with political violence? You think I wouldn't burn this city to the ground to rid it of its corruption and foreign filth?" His tone remained conversational. "Silvestri's got some little Englishman of his own working for him – he isn't going to last much longer. And you... You really should have listened to me."

"Well, I'm ready to let it go," Daniel said. "Wherever it is, I don't think I'm going to find it."

Mario sat up slightly straighter.

"That's something, coming from the great Daniel Taylor," he said. "Our climate doesn't suit you, perhaps?"

Daniel smiled. "No. It doesn't. I'm going to let the Russian know that I've quit. Once I've done that, he's out of the game. Silvestri isn't even in the game. The ring remains lost. It means that your guys can stop shooting people."

The other man watched him in silence.

"Why should I believe you?" he asked finally.

Daniel shrugged. "That's up to you," he said. He pulled himself to his feet. He could feel sweat beginning to trickle down his neck. This, he realised, would be the moment. And then, from the darkness behind him, came a deep, irate voice.

"Don't fucking move, Dottore. Put your hands up."

Daniel turned to see two men striding towards Mario. One, a neatly-dressed man wearing a tie, and the other, the man who had spoken, grey and shaven-headed. Each of them held a gun.

Mario slowly rose from the bench. He said levelly, "You guys are making a mistake."

"Walk towards me," the shaven-headed man said. "Shut up and keep your hands up." He gestured his gun casually in Daniel's direction. "And you, get lost. Now."

As Daniel moved away, leaning on his crutch, there was a sudden explosion of gunfire from the trees beyond the bench. So Mario did have a friend with him.

Both men hit the ground with practised speed. The shaven-headed man pulled Mario down on top of him, and put his gun to his head.

"I'll blow his brains out," he roared. "Watch me!" The gunfire from the trees became sporadic, and hesitant, and stopped. "That's fucking better," the shaven-headed man said. He noticed Daniel, who had moved cautiously into the shadow of the trees. "I told you to get lost," he barked, as he hauled Mario back onto his feet.

Mario smiled. "You morons are going to regret this," he said.

The shaven-headed man cuffed him across the head. Daniel began to back away.

"And so are you, you treacherous English scum," Mario shouted after him. "You're a dead man."

Daniel was close to a set of steps that led steeply down to the road. As he began to feel his way down them his crutch slipped, and he fell heavily, head first. The earth struck him like a fist, and he lay momentarily stunned, his injured leg jolted into fierce new pain. He could hear more gunfire from above him. He pulled himself with agonising care down the remaining slippery stone steps, a taste of blood in his mouth. He edged towards his crutch which was lying on the pavement below him. It took him a long time to reach it, and by the time he did, he realised that the night had become quiet again. Somehow, he'd survived.

Chapter Thirty-Eight

Dan stepped outside into the velvety darkness and inhaled the scent of pines. The gravelled drive swept down to electronically controlled gates, and these swung silently open at his approach.

So it was true. He was free.

It was a strange moment. He was still wearing his chinos and trainers. He badly needed a shave. He had no money. He inhaled again, breathing in all the sweetness of the world. In the distance, across Rome's rolling hillsides, Dan could see the lights of the city. He had no idea how far away it was. He followed the road which wound very gradually down the hill, and eventually managed to hitch a ride. It was an old van driven by a boy of about seventeen, who smoked cigarettes and was utterly indifferent to him. It seemed to Dan that he'd only given him a lift in order to show off his ability to drive one-handed and very fast whilst being bored. They reached the outskirts of the city, and the boy pulled up abruptly. Clearly his ride ended here.

"Grazie," Dan said, as he dismounted.

The boy said something that sounded like "Niente," and then Dan walked again.

It was one o'clock in the morning before he finally arrived back at his hotel. He was exhausted, with a bleeding blister on one heel.

The receptionist said, "Good evening, Mr Taylor," as he passed the desk, and he took the lift up to his suite, and opened the door. He was so overwhelmed with relief that all he could do was sink onto a chair. He was back. He could shower and then lie down on his fresh, comfortable bed. He felt as if he could stay there forever. He poured himself a glass of cold water, and sipped it, tasting it as if he had never drunk water before. He could, of course, now book another flight, and get himself back home. But, on the other hand, the reasons he had for leaving the city had now disappeared. Now, he realised, he could return to his course, and see Eva, and Ellie, and Mitchell, and Dell, and Todd. Silvestri's men no longer mattered. Dan took a malt whisky from his mini bar and mixed it with a little water. He drank with a sense of cleansing himself of fear, and helplessness, and self-loathing. He was back.

And he woke the next morning to a knock on the door.

"Room service, Signor Taylor."

"Thank you. Grazie."

A breakfast tray of fresh orange juice, cappuccino, and two large cornetti, with blackcurrant jam, was placed beside him, still drowsy, in his giant bed. He couldn't quite believe that he'd ordered himself breakfast in bed, but he had. How fantastic. Outside, it was a clear blue day, and he could hear the distant traffic and energy of a Rome morning. He lay back on his pillows. Every mad, scary, and demoralising thing that had happened since he found Piero on his balcony in the early morning could now be safely and quietly stowed away.

His phone was working. He would text his brother, perhaps even text Jack, wanker that he was, and get on with being a visitor in this stupendous city. He could, had he wished, have had a deep jacuzzi bubble bath, but he settled for a hot shower and a shave. He felt surprisingly okay. This was probably partly because he no longer had Piero looking at him speculatively, and Silvestri calling him a fool, but also partly because he'd managed to survive the whole thing, and had slept like one dead.

He arrived early at the lecture room, and Eva was there, preparing her slides. She smiled when she saw him, and embraced him.

"I'm glad you're back," she said. "Silvestri, really..." She shook her head. "The man's an outrage."

This too made Dan feel better. He may not have acquitted himself particularly well, but none of this had been his fault, after all. And when his fellow students arrived, he found that he was still basking in the glow of having been responsible for them all visiting the Silvestri palazzo. It was almost unbelievable that he had only seen them all two days ago. It felt as if another lifetime had passed since then.

Today, at last, the Vatican Museums and the Sistine Chapel. He could not have timed his return better. This was how it felt to have briefly faced death – a renewed gratitude for the splendour of life, and an appreciation of everyone, even Dell.

Mitchell shook his hand. "Good to see you again," he said. His bright, quizzical eyes rested on his face. "Let's grab a beer later, and you can tell me what you've been up to."

"Sure." Dan nodded, feeling something like affection for Mitchell. Eva's lecture was crisp and informative, and then they left the Museum, and headed for the Metro. This, too, was an adventure. They joined the crowds descending the stairs, and shuffled their way along to the platform. Their stop was Ottaviano, and they emerged into sunshine.

They had time, before visiting the Museums, to walk down to St Peter's Square and look at the basilica. On one side of the wide road was a sombre, blank wall, behind which stood anonymous Vatican buildings. On the other side were shops selling memorabilia and plastic aprons and keyrings. Street sellers had displays of fake designer handbags set out on sheets on the pavement. There was also a roast chestnut vendor, and various stalls selling hats and sunglasses.

Eva, wearing an ID card on a ribbon, sternly marched them all past the bars, rosary beads, and Vatican guides offering tours. The wide square was crowded with international visitors, all taking photographs of the basilica and each other, and Dan counted nuns. There was a festive atmosphere that matched his mood, and for once he was quite happy to be herded. He even posed for a group photograph in front of one of the fountains. Then they joined the long queue, and finally entered the enormous church.

For Dan, a secular man, it was a curious experience. It seemed to him that vastness and spirituality were quite possibly not the same thing. St Peters was gloomy, and somehow chilling. He felt that its massive, glowering quality was very similar to that of the Colosseum. Having gone in, he would have been perfectly happy to just come straight out again. But he stayed with the others, peering at angels and dead popes, and maintaining a suitably respectful expression.

"Now this is just majestic," Mitchell murmured approvingly.

Finally they were able to escape into the sunshine again, and then, after coffee, they were ready for the museums. They walked through the centuries of art, losing and finding one another again in the eddying mass of visitors. Dan stopped before a collection of pale blue angels, feeling suddenly and inexplicably close to tears. St Sebastian raised his eyes to heaven, his white body punctured bloodlessly by arrows. In vast canvases, God the Father, with Jesus at his right hand, occupied the top level, while below them popes and bishops busied themselves with His work. The certainty and authority of all of these works was both impressive and strange.

And all the time they edged closer to the Sistine Chapel. The crowds thickened and slowed as they wound through the corridors and chambers that would lead them there. There was a growing air of anticipation, and Dan divided his attention between the pictures and frescoes they were passing, and his Blue Guide. Signs assured them that they were heading in the right direction. Their group gradually intermingled with a large party of friendly Germans, and they chatted, and shuffled, and peered ahead.

By the time they reached the entrance, Dan realised that he was holding his breath. The Chapel itself was a sea of people, and descending its steps felt like stepping onto a stockmarket floor on a particularly busy afternoon.

"Bit of a scrum, isn't it?" Mitchell muttered, putting his glasses on, the better to inspect the walls. The din of conversation reverberated through the chapel. Staff would occasionally call for silence, and the hubbub would reduce to a murmur, before steadily rising again. Cameras and mobile phones flashed, despite the ban on photography.

Dan wound his way through the crowds. It was difficult to get a clear view, and he was distracted by the need to look up, keep moving, and avoid walking into other people. Finally he gained a seat on the bench which ran all the way round the walls. He was at the far end of the room from the Judgment. He gazed at the saved and the damned, and tried to be drawn into this naked world of hope and despair. Overhead, God was reaching out to Adam, and the Bible whirled around in magnificent coloured segments.

I'm here, Dan thought. Now. I'm really inside the Sistine Chapel.

He concentrated on ignoring the bustle all around him and absorbing the complicated ceiling. He only half listened when Mitchell spoke to him, and it took a little while for his urgent words to sink in:

"Dan. There's a guy over there been taking your photograph."

When he looked over, following the direction of Mitchell's nod, the man had gone.

Chapter Thirty-Nine

"Sorry, Daniel. I fell asleep waiting for you." Alessandro, awake and dishevelled, rolled off Daniel's bed. "You slept on the sofa?"

"It's okay, Alessandro," Daniel said. He had started to gather his few things together.

"Daniel, what's happened to you? Someone hit you?" Alessandro peered at Daniel's face. "You need some ice for your forehead – that's a big bruise. Nasty."

"I'm okay," Daniel said. "It's time for me to go, Alessandro."

"What?" Alessandro gasped. "Daniel – what are you doing? You can't go yet."

"I think I need to," he said.

"Nonsense, Daniel. We have more work to do!"

"We do?"

"Certainly. I told you. You know about our brother Luca?"

"The one you don't talk to?"

Alessandro was horrified. "You mean I didn't tell you? I meant to tell you last night. My God." He shook his head and sat down on the bed again. "Daniel, listen to me. We've discussed this very carefully. The only one who could have had access to the bank vault is our brother. He's a very self-centred person. And probably a little crazy. Well, except that he never trusted Mariaurora, and he could have been right... I know she's dead, and of course that's a tragedy, but... Well, you met her."

Daniel waited for this to go somewhere.

"And then we remembered that Luca visited Rome, out of the blue, a few years ago. Livia and I didn't see him – he's a very difficult man – but he went to see Mariaurora." His intense blue eyes rested on Daniel. "You see? I don't think

Mariaurora would have lied to us about the ring. But Luca... certainly. Certainly. And he needed money. His rich wife was divorcing him, and his business needed money. It was laughable."

"What is his business?"

"He's a dealer in military artefacts. It's one business where our family history helps." Alessandro gave a gloomy shrug. "And he'd have known much better than us what the ring of Diocletian is worth. So – do you think that visit was an innocent trip, just to catch up with his dear sister Mariaurora?"

Daniel felt a massive weariness settling over him.

"Where does Luca live?" he asked.

"Manchester," Alessandro replied.

"What – Manchester, England?"

Alessandro nodded.

"I've booked us tickets," he said. "Our flight leaves at midday."

Chapter Forty

Dan felt that he had been abruptly doused in ice-cold water. Fear, all the more powerful for being uncertain, swept over him. Who...? And what was he supposed to do? Suddenly the noise, the crowds, and the intensity of Michelangelo's work, all combined to make him feel faint. He needed to get out.

Mitchell said, "Are you okay, Dan? You look a little pale."

"I'm not feeling... very good," he replied, and allowed Mitchell to steer him out of the Chapel and into the café, where he sipped a glass of very cold water, and began to recover.

"It's pretty close in there," Mitchell said. "Take your time. You probably just need some air."

"It isn't that," Dan whispered. "I think I might be in trouble."

"Really?" Mitchell almost visibly brightened. "Tell me." He stood up. "In fact, let's get out of here and get a drink."

Dan unquestioningly followed him out of the Vatican and up onto Via Cola del Rienza, where they found a bar and Mitchell ordered them both caffè corretto – literally, corrected coffee – which was espresso with their choice of alcohol. Dan chose brandy, spooned sugar on top, and told Mitchell the whole story.

"Wow," the Canadian said, with an unmistakeable note of envy. "What a time you've been having."

"Mitchell, I don't know what to do."

Mitchell considered. "Well, someone is interested in you. But probably not Silvestri, since he let you go. Right?"

Dan nodded. "I think so. He thinks I'm..." He trailed off. "Not very significant."

"Okay. So the other guy is this Mario guy. A university academic, you said?" Dan could hear the slight note of scepticism in Mitchell's voice.

"A very aggressive academic," he said.

"Well, if he's got a problem with you because of Silvestri, maybe you could get some protection from Silvestri? Why don't you call his guys, Piero and Stefan?"

"I don't have their numbers," Dan said. He had downed his coffee in one, and now gestured for another. "And anyway, they're dangerous." He took a sip of his second coffee. "And they wouldn't care," he concluded, a little sadly. "And neither would Silvestri." An old, familiar weight of unhappiness and helplessness had resettled on his shoulders. "I think I need to get out of here," he said. "I just need to… go home."

Mitchell considered this.

"Maybe it isn't such a good idea for you to go home just yet," he said. "If this Mario character has connections, they may be able to trace your address."

"Really?"

"Sure. It isn't difficult. So it might be an idea for you to not be there for a while." He pondered further. "Do you have anyone you could stay with? What about your brother? Where does he live?"

"Boston," Dan said. "But… Do you really think…?"

Mitchell was about to reply when someone caught his eye.

"Dan, don't look behind you," he said quietly, "but I see that guy…"

Dan wrenched his head around, just as a quiet, intent young man who was standing at the counter, wearing a dark jacket and a black v-neck jumper, drained his cup. He blinked under Dan's alarmed gaze.

"Not him," Mitchell hissed. "Don't…"

But Dan craned his neck further, and this time he noticed two men who had come in a few minutes after them and taken up places at the end of the bar. Casually dressed, nondescript, fairly young. They hadn't ordered coffee.

Mitchell said, "The one on the left is the guy who was taking your picture in the Sistine Chapel. They see that you've noticed them. Listen, Dan. We are going to leave now, okay? We are going to go back to your hotel to get your things. We are going to stay in very public, very crowded places, and we are going to stay together. Got all that?"

Dan nodded.

"Okay," Mitchell said. "Let's go."

He slid casually off his seat, and, followed by Dan, walked out of the bar and onto the wide, busy road. A child with an ice cream, an elderly man playing the violin, a strolling couple with shopping bags. Dan dodged round them all and was then stopped by Mitchell touching his arm.

"Dan, which direction is your hotel?"

"Oh…"

He turned round, so that he was facing in the right direction. He couldn't see the men. Maybe this was all a mistake. A false alarm. This could quite possibly all be a false alarm. He was now following Mitchell, who, while seemingly strolling along the pavement, was actually moving fairly quickly.

They reached the end of Via Cola del Rienza, and crossed a bridge. Ahead of them, the wall of the wide Piazza del Popolo, with Egyptian obelisk and fountains. To one side, the church of Santa Maria dei Popolo, home to two Caravaggios. Dan had meant to visit it… Now, they started along one of the crowded roads that led off the Piazza, and Dan saw that this was the famous Via del Corso, choked with people strolling and gazing into shop windows.

He realised that he'd lost Mitchell in the crowd. He kept moving, stepping out into the road to get round shuffling tourists, and then stepping back onto the pavement as traffic went past. This was a definition of hell. He paused at a crossroads and looked back. A milling multitude of faces met him, and he scanned them carefully.

And there they were, some way back, the two men. They seemed to be in no hurry, walking side by side up the road, stopping to let people go past them, calm and impassive. But Dan had spent enough time with Piero and Stefan to recognise this kind of professionalism. He felt his heart beginning to pound. What if he had a heart attack, right here, in the middle of Via del Corso? Panic was beginning to fog him. He couldn't, he just couldn't, keep fighting his way through this crowd... The men were going to catch up with him, it was only a matter of time...

And where the hell was Mitchell? He'd vanished as if he'd been a ghost amongst the tangle of people and shopping bags and cars and buses and motorbikes and street performers and an amorphous mass of French schoolchildren who were all wearing red baseball caps and backpacks and drifting along as one never-ending obstacle. Dan took a couple of deep breaths. He had to just keep going. Keep going. Back to his hotel on Via Nazionale, and then the airport.

Suddenly Mitchell was beside him again, as if he hadn't been lost at all.

"When we get to Vittorio Emanuele I'm going to try to head them off," he said briskly. "You just go for it. Just take your passport and your credit card – it's all you need."

Dan simply nodded, and concentrated on moving and breathing at the same time. At the end of Via del Corso was the hugely complicated Piazza Venezia, where traffic streamed and pedestrians crossed over to the vast white monument to the Emperor Vittorio Emanuele II. Even by Rome's excessive standards, it had seemed to Dan, this was an insanely ornate building, from the chariots on its roof to the bronze groups at the foot of its wide steps. He skirted round it. Had Mitchell managed to distract his pursuers? He had no idea. He knew that he needed to continue along this road, Via Alessandrina, and then head up Via Cavour and turn onto one of the roads that would lead him through to Via Nationale... Easy.

Just keep walking. Quickly.

Chapter Forty-One

The wind at Manchester Airport bit through Daniel's coat and froze his ears.

"English weather. My God," muttered Alessandro, who had dressed for the journey in fur hat, scarf, and overcoat.

They emerged into the grey afternoon and Alessandro produced his brother's address. Their taxi driver swung out into the traffic and Daniel cautiously flexed his injured leg, which was hurting more than usual in the cold, and watched as they made their way into the city. Alessandro was uncharacteristically quiet, and just stared out of the window.

Finally the taxi drew up outside an old house that stood behind a deep, shaggy privet hedge. The windows were blanked out by blinds, and a For Sale sign hung at an angle from the front door. Daniel climbed carefully out of the taxi, and Alessandro tried to pay the driver in euros. While Daniel found enough sterling to cover the fare, the Italian rang his brother.

"Luca. We're here. We're outside."

Silence. The road itself was quiet and tree-lined, and Daniel noted the leaves in bud, and the splashes of yellow where primroses were beginning to blossom in gardens. From somewhere, the sound of a car alarm bleeping was carried on the breeze. The air was damp with coming rain, and as they stood, the wind began to rise.

"Jesus Christ," Alessandro said, producing a large, dark green umbrella. "Jesus, Daniel, what a country."

Daniel said, "Did you get through?"

"No," Alessandro replied tersely. "Just voicemail." They both looked at the house.

"Do you think he's here?" Daniel asked.

Alessandro muttered something dark, and strode on up the

path to ring the bell. While Daniel waited, an elderly man, wearing a pair of gardening gloves, straightened up from his roses in the next door garden.

"Hello there!" he called. "Can I help you?"

Alessandro just glared at him, but Daniel said, "We were hoping to find Luca."

"Ah." The man nodded. "He moved out a little while ago."

"This is his brother," Daniel said, as Alessandro stomped down the path again.

"Yes – I see the resemblance," the man said cheerfully, and walked down to his front gate, taking off his gloves in order to shake hands with them. "Well, I'd guess the best place to find him is at the lock-up, where he keeps his stock."

"You don't have an address…?"

"Absolutely. Just a moment, and I'll get it." The man went back into his house.

Alessandro said, "You see? He moves house and doesn't tell anyone. I'm telling you, Daniel, he's devious. You'll see."

The neighbour came back with a yellow Post-It note.

"He left this with me, in case any customers called. I'm sure he'll be delighted to see you," he added, to Alessandro.

The Italian gave a non-committal nod. "Thank you," he said finally.

"You're welcome," the man said, and returned to his garden.

The lock-up was in an area of dilapidated garages and workshops, and Daniel and Alessandro spent some time wandering along irregular rows of doors, none of which were numbered, while heavy, single drops of rain fell. Alessandro had by now left several more messages on Luca's phone. His mood had darkened to a point where he was no longer speaking.

This suited Daniel, low as he was on ideas and hope. The afternoon was becoming evening, and he let Alessandro stride ahead while he counted units, and tried to work out where Luca's, 17A, was likely to be. And then, just as darkness began to make their search impossible, a wooden door opened and light streamed out. At last – someone to ask.

Alessando quickened his pace, in case the door should close again before they got there. And then a shout of triumph.

"Daniel! He's here!"

Daniel approached the door, where the two brothers were now standing in the harsh light of the lock-up. They didn't embrace or shake hands. Luca was of similar height, build and swagger to Alessandro. He was slightly older, and possibly slightly more bear-like, dressed in faded jeans and a thick jumper. His eyes moved from his brother to Daniel.

Finally he said, "I'm busy."

Alessandro nodded.

"I can see that, Luca." He idly picked up a pair of flying goggles and tossed them contemptuously back. "Still dealing in this junk. I wonder sometimes just what happened to you."

Luca said, "You're a drunk and a cretin, Alessandro. Go back to Rome."

Daniel, propped on his crutch, said, "I wonder if we could all perhaps sit down somewhere?"

Luca sighed. Then he said, "There's a pub near here. We could go there as long as he," indicating his brother, "behaves himself."

"You see?" Alessandro said to Daniel. "Insults and abuse. That's all he has for his family."

"Shut up, Alessandro," Luca said, closing the door. They made their way to the end of the path by means of his torch. And there, almost invisible amongst the trees, was a small pub, The Rabbit Catcher, with a dim light shining through the windows. Inside, a jukebox was playing Elvis Presley. It was empty of customers. The woman behind the bar looked up from her book of crosswords.

"Yes, love?"

"Three bottles of Newcastle Brown," Luca said. "There's no point ordering anything else here," he added, as he steered them to a table away from the door. He got up again to bring over the bottles and glasses, and they all poured their drinks.

Alessandro said, "Did Livia let you know about

Mariaurora?"

Luca nodded, looking suitably sombre.

"You know why she was killed?"

Luca shrugged. "A break-in, I guess. A thief. You think there's a mystery?"

"She was killed for the ring," Alessandro said, leaning forward for emphasis.

"What ring?"

Alessandro gave Daniel a look. My brother the snake, the look said. Luca seemed completely unmoved and took a mouthful of brown ale.

"The ring of Diocletian," Alessandro said. "Benito's ring. You know what ring."

"Mariaurora never had the ring," Luca said. "She had a copy."

Alessandro stared at him. "You knew? You knew?"

Luca had evidently decided to ignore his younger brother, and instead spoke to Daniel.

"I saw it years ago. Mariaurora wanted to sell it, to fund her church work, and she asked me to value it for her."

"But she had no right…"

"Please, Alessandro. So I went over and had a look at it, but I knew it wasn't the real thing. The ring of Diocletian would be worth a small fortune. Why would it have come to us?"

"And you didn't say anything?"

"I told Mariaurora, but you know what she was like. Of course she didn't believe me. She thought I was part of some anti-God conspiracy. So I just came back here. But I noticed that she didn't try to sell it, so obviously she didn't want to test her faith in it too far." He drained his glass. "When are you going back to Rome?"

"Tonight," Alessandro said. "We have a flight at nine o'clock."

Luca glanced at his watch.

"Say hello to Livia for me," he said. "And Agnese."

Alessandro said, "Who has the ring, Luca?"

Luca shrugged. "I have no idea. You think I have it? You

think I took it from Mariaurora and left her with a copy?" He gestured to Daniel. "Look at him. That's what he thinks. Alessandro, ask yourself. Would I have had to sell my house, and be working out of a lock-up in Levenshulme, if I'd got the ring of Diocletian?" He drained his glass. "I'm busy. I've got a fair tomorrow at Alderley Edge." He stood up, and, finally, he put his hand out to his brother. "Safe journey, Alessandro."

Alessandro hesitated, but returned the handshake.

"That was our legacy," he said. "It's been stolen from us, and I'm going to find it."

Luca shook his head. "It never was. Come on. Think about our family. Think about Benito's death. You don't think someone grabbed the ring? Of course someone grabbed it. And probably sold it. But I don't know who, and I don't know when. And strangely enough – I don't care. You're right about this stuff, Alessandro – it is junk. It's all junk. Benito was a monster. We're better off without a legacy from him."

A melancholy silence fell. The jukebox played Love Me Tender.

Daniel said, "Come on, Alessandro. You need to get to the airport. I need to get to the station."

The rain had become steady and heavy as they sped back through Manchester. Daniel took a call from the Russian.

"No," he said. "I've found nothing in Rome. I'm taking the train back to London…"

Alessandro stared at him. When he'd finished the call he said, "You're not coming back to Rome?"

He shook his head.

"But you're British," Alessandro pointed out reproachfully. "Where's your bulldog spirit?"

Daniel smiled. "I don't think I have much of that left."

"Daniel, you must come back. We have more searching to do… Livia will never forgive me if I go back without you. And what about Sophia? She saved your life, and you're not even going to say goodbye to her?"

Daniel hesitated. "I'm not helping the situation over

there," he said. "I don't want anyone else to get killed."

"Nonsense," Alessandro said. "My God, Daniel – look at this weather. This will kill you. You can't stay here. Come back with me, and then decide. Talk to your brother."

They were now at Piccadilly Station, its lights shimmering through the water that ran down the taxi windows.

"Daniel," Alessandro said, "it isn't over yet."

Chapter Forty-Two

They were gaining on him. In a leisurely way, without even seeming to try. Dan's pace had quickened from fast to extremely fast. He was darting past milling groups of tourists, ice-cream sellers, souvenir sellers, Centurions in full costume, the Colosseo Metro Station... It was only here that he realised he'd gone too far. Quite a long way too far. He'd completely missed the turn for Via Cavour. He doubled back and into the Metro. He could get a train... That would lose them... He threw money into the machine and snatched his ticket. Then the barrier. A pause while his ticket was rejected. A nice Japanese nun showed him how to put it in the right way, and then through the gates, down the stairs, onto the platform... and straight onto a train. Brilliant. Luck. He had no idea which direction it was going in, but that didn't matter. He suddenly noticed, with a frisson of fear, that the train didn't have doors between the carriages.

What kind of train was this? It stretched away, with everyone on it perfectly visible to anyone following them... He picked up the paper that had been left on his seat, and opened it wide. He peered from behind it, and yes, there they were. Standing, relaxed, in conversation, about two carriages down. He was trapped. The train had been a bad idea.

He opened the paper wider, ignoring the glare of the woman sitting next to him, and scanned the line map over the doors. The next stop was Termini. Okay. Perfect. That was the main rail and bus station. He'd get off there, he could walk to his hotel from there, or get a cab, and there'd be crowds of people... A group of tall American teenagers, all talking and laughing quite loudly, had congregated round the door. He just needed to time things so that he was camouflaged by them.

And he did. Up, out, onto the platform, with American voices all around him. He was carried by the crowd towards the exit and the escalators. He was still holding the newspaper. He was doing pretty well. There was no question of running up the escalators – they were solid with people – but he felt increasingly safe, surrounded by anonymous humanity, as he followed signs for the exit. It wasn't until he had reached the main station, and moved past its coffee bars, bookshop, ticket office, and people with cases, that Dan realised that the two men were still behind him.

It brought him to a brief halt of pure panic. Then he ran. Outside, the day was bright and cool, and he had no idea which direction to head in. He raced along the side of the building. And it was then that he noticed the heaps of sleeping bags and huddled figures, down towards the back of the station.

Something he had once read in John Buchan's The Thirty-Nine Steps suddenly came back to him across the decades: to disguise yourself, you need to become part of your landscape. There was a man asleep on his side under a blanket, only his dirty bare feet visible, and an open sleeping bag, with a crumpled sports bag as a pillow, next to him. Obviously whoever had been lying there had got up, and would probably be coming back... But that didn't matter. Dan sat down on the empty sleeping bag, and then lay down. He pulled a soiled pink blanket over himself. He would wait. He would just wait until dark. And he cautiously stretched out, propping his head on one elbow. The man next to him was so still that Dan began to fear that he was dead.

The smell of the blanket was of McDonald's and sweat. Initially it had been hardly noticeable, but as time went on it became more and more dominant. Dan could see, at a curious angle, the whole sweep of the road up to the station's corner, and the legs and feet of everyone who went past. No sign of the two men. He slowly eased the blanket down from his face. He should think of this as a chess game. He should work out what they would do next, and then do something to counter it. But he had no idea what the men might do. He had no idea what he should do. He wasn't even sure how to get to Via Nazionale from here. The hardness of the pavement under the sleeping bag was beginning to hurt his back. It would be hours and hours before it was dark.

And what if the owner of the sleeping bag came back? What if the man next to him woke up? But there was nothing he could do except stay very, very still.

And so he lay his head down and waited.

Chapter Forty-Three

It was a clear night in Rome. Daniel, unable to sleep, watched the moon as it moved slowly across the sky. He'd had a late dinner with his brother. Julian had frowned, and picked at his salad.

"You're right, of course," he said. "You are part of the problem." He fixed his younger brother with his chilly eyes. "But not the whole problem. This is taking on its own momentum, and we need, if we can, to check it with minimum bloodshed." He sighed. "I've been charged by the Vatican to do anything possible to stop further violence here in Rome. And perhaps broker some kind of an agreement between the parties. Unofficially." He sipped his wine. "Is there anything you can think of that might help me?"

Daniel shook his head. "The Russian's just fixated on the ring. He did…" Daniel remembered something. "He did text me, and sent me a photograph. Apparently these are the men Silvestri used to kill his man." He flicked through his phone. Julian studied the blurred image carefully.

He said, "That man in the middle… I can't be quite sure, but I believe I've met him. I met him at Silvestri's villa. He's actually a tourist – the one who got confused with you, because of his name. And the Russian thinks he's one of Silvestri's men?"

"Apparently. He warned me to look out for them. He thinks they're the ones who shot me. He's wrong, and I told him he was, but he doesn't listen."

"Do you know who shot you?" Julian asked.

He nodded. "There's a neo-fascist group that wants the ring."

Julian considered. "That would make sense."

They ate in silence. Daniel drank a glass of wine.

"None of this is good," Julian said, finally.

"No," Daniel agreed.

Julian raised his hand for their bill. "Except, I suppose, that we've been able to have dinner together," he added. "Sleep well, Daniel. And let's stay in touch."

He had let himself into the house, careful not to disturb Alessandro, who was banging about in the cellars, and slowly made his way up the stairs to his room. On his own phone, a message from Sabato: Daniel, please come. It's urgent. Very urgent. And a PS: It wasn't safe in London. I was being staked out by some creep.

Emil, Daniel guessed. He called him.

"Daniel, I can't talk on the phone," Sabato said, his voice low and anxious. "Just come."

"Where are you?"

"Boston."

"Boston ?"

"I've got a friend at the University here. I'm staying with him and his wife."

"Sabato, the situation has changed. I've quit. I'm not going to look for the ring any more."

"What? What are you talking about? Daniel, you can't quit."

"I have. I can't help you, Sabato."

"Jesus, Daniel. I need you here. You're the only one who can make this okay with the Russian. Please." An anxious silence. "Daniel, just come."

And he hesitated. It was very unlikely that he could make anything okay with the Russian any more. But, even so, he found that he couldn't quite let go, although he knew that he should.

Now, the night hours drifted. His flight was booked, his bag packed. He would explain to the family in the morning, before his taxi arrived. He watched the branches of the trees in the garden shifting restlessly, and heard the sound of a cat somewhere, howling at the sky.

He had begun to doze, and was startled when a tap came on his door. Sophia appeared.

"Daniel, I think there's someone in the garden."
"Isn't there a police guard there?"
She shook her head.
"He was called away this evening. A murder in Baldo degli Ubaldi." She perched on the bed. "I've called the police, and they said they'd be here as soon as they could... But I don't know how long that will be..."

"Even though your boyfriend's a detective?" He intended it to be a joke, but somehow it didn't come out like that.

Sophia said, "Daniel, Emiliano is a friend of mine. I used to work with him. He has a very nice wife called Laura, and a beautiful son called Christiano. I'm Christiano's godmother." She looked at him sternly. "So. No boyfriend." She glanced at the room. "Do I take it that you're thinking of disappearing again?"

She was sitting close beside him. He smelt her scent, noticed again the pattern of freckles across her nose, the shine of her lips, the gleam of her teeth. She was wearing a baggy tracksuit but underneath he could guess the outline of her shoulders, her breasts, her waist. He could feel the warmth of her body. He was about to speak, to say something, although he wasn't quite sure what, when suddenly from downstairs came a sound like an explosion.

Sophia said, "I'll be back," and headed for the corridor.

There was an answering explosion from outside the house – a gunshot. Daniel picked up his crutch and left his room, swinging himself down the stairs. Alessandro was at the front door, holding a shotgun, with a look of sheer exhilaration on his face.

"You heard that?" he asked Sophia. "Livia said it was my imagination, but I know an intruder when I see one. Lurking about in the gardens."

"You shot at him?" Sophia asked incredulously.

"Certainly," Alessandro said. "No point in pussy-footing around. And he's shot back. So now..."

He opened the front door just wide enough to fit the muzzle of the gun, and let off another shot. The noise temporarily made speech impossible. Another shot from outside, and a bullet thudded into the heavy wood of the door as Alessandro slammed it shut. He whistled with relish.

"We have a fight on our hands," he said. "Come, Daniel, I have another shotgun in the cellar. Can you shoot? I'll show you."

Livia appeared, wrapped in a heavy jade silk dressing-gown, both frightened and exasperated.

"Daniel, Sophia, stop him. He's a madman. He'll get us all killed."

"The police will be here soon," Sophia said. "Alessandro, don't open the door again. Put the rifle down."

But Alessandro was already inching open the door, and a bullet howled through the air as he did so and shaved a piece of wood from the edge as he slammed it shut again.

"Wow." His face was radiant. "Okay – into the front room," he said. "We can shoot from the window. Daniel, come on!" He crossed the hall and flung open the doors of an evidently unused room, evading Livia's attempt to grab his arm.

Sophia said "Maybe we should stay with him... If the shooter gets into the house... Where's Agnese?"

"Asleep," Livia said. "She takes tablets."

"We need to be together," Sophia said. "I'll get her."

The front room was huge and largely bare, with dark-streaked walls and a mildewed ceiling dominated by an enormous candelabra. Its windows looked out over the dark tangle of the front gardens, only one corner lit by the moon. Alessandro had smashed a hole in the base of one of the windows and was crouching on the floor, with the barrel of the gun sticking through the broken glass above him.

Livia said, "Come back over here, Alessandro. Stop being ridiculous."

"I'm defending my house," her brother replied, raising his head cautiously to peer through the glass. "And I'm defending my family."

"It's probably me they're trying to shoot, not you," Daniel said.

"I wouldn't be too sure about that," Alessandro said. "You

know I'm writing a book about Silvestri? An exposé? It's going to be a bomb. A bomb. This is his way of trying to silence me. As if I can be silenced."

Sophia and Agnese came in, Agnese with her hair tied roughly into a topknot, and wearing an oversize towelling robe. They joined Daniel and Livia in the corner of the room furthest away from where Alessandro had just fired again, the sound reverberating and setting the glass of the candelabra tinkling.

"Nothing," he said, disappointed, raising his head again to peer out into the gardens.

"Thank God for that," Livia said. "Alessandro, stop this now."

But her brother was once again aiming into the darkness.

Chapter Forty-Four

The man stirred him with a foot, quite gently. He was a small, gaunt figure wearing an LA Raiders sweatshirt and a shapeless dark anorak. He was quite young, his hair harshly cut into a very short, spiky fringe.

Dan scrambled to his feet. He had no idea of the protocol of this situation, so he stepped away from the sleeping bag and said, "Thank you. Grazie. Ciao."

The man nodded, clearly puzzled, and sat down. The sleeping figure alongside remained still.

It was evening. The sunset was fading, and Dan was cold now that he was no longer covered by the pink blanket. He'd drifted off to sleep a couple of times, into strange dreams in which his back hurt, and had then almost instantly woken again to find that not only his back, but his shoulders, elbows, and knees were all hurting. Now, he experimentally bent his legs and tried his feet, while the man in the sleeping bag watched him. There were other rough sleepers lying in protective rows against the side of the building, travellers arriving and departing, lights shining from shops and bars, and buses and trams passing by. There was a smell of fried chicken coming from somewhere.

Dan had to get back to his hotel. He just had to. He peered cautiously around, but he couldn't see any sign of his pursuers. He began to walk through the dim evening light, and as he moved he began to feel a certain confidence returning, despite the pain in his lower back. He'd thrown them off. He'd become part of his landscape. He ran his hands through his hair, which seemed to be sticking up, and wove his way through the early evening crowds and street sellers. He put the coins in his pocket into the cup of a beggar.

But, as he approached the doors of his hotel, some instinct slowed him. The doorman was about to throw the door open for him, but he shook his head in quick entreaty, and instead peered through the glass. Was there…?

There was. A young, nondescript guy slumped on one of the leather sofas, looking down at his phone. Dan backed away. The doorman watched him in silence. He walked quickly down the road. He needed to pee. He needed to eat. He needed his money and his passport. He felt like weeping. But a number of half-forgotten movies came drifting back to him. Movies in which heroes made their way up fire-exit steps, or through kitchens…

It should be possible. It shouldn't be beyond him. The back of the building was on another street, and he wandered along it, eyeing up the smooth, high walls. The occasional gate he came to was firmly locked. Lights shone from high up, far away windows, like a vision of paradise lost. God. Was he going to have to sleep out here all night? He couldn't. He just couldn't.

He walked again along the walls. Inside, in the kitchens, there would be an army of staff cutting, chopping, steaming, frying, and in the hotel's bars and dining rooms the first of the evening's guests would be sipping aperitivi, and relaxing. He hated them. He hated all of them. He was cold. Hungry. Tired. He had by now walked right around the building, and back to the front of the hotel. He wondered if he could just peer through the glass again. But the doorman blocked his path.

"May I assist you, sir?" he asked in perfect English. Dan retreated. The doorman followed him. "May I assist you?" he asked again, more sternly. Dan shook his head.

"No," he said.

"Do you wish to enter the hotel?" the doorman asked.

"No. Well, yes. But…" Could he explain his situation to the doorman? "I do want to enter the hotel. The problem is —"

"Are you a guest in this hotel?" the doorman asked.

He nodded. "I am a guest in this hotel. But I have a big

problem."

A well-dressed, middle-aged couple came out, smiled briefly at the doorman, glanced at Dan, and then walked away. A French family arrived, and the doorman opened the door for them with a flourish. Then he turned wordlessly back to Dan.

"I'm waiting for someone," Dan said. He'd realised that he couldn't explain his situation to this man. The doorman gave a slight nod. He was maintaining a veneer of courtesy, but his nod seemed to incorporate disbelief, distain, and an unstated warning. He swivelled away from Dan to open the door for a tall cleric who was about to enter. The cleric, however, stopped.

"Mr Taylor," he said. "I'm pleased to see you. How are you?"

Dan looked at him blankly for a minute, and then remembered. Silvestri's villa.

"I'm... kind of in trouble," Dan said.

The cleric inclined his head. "So it appears," he said. "I thought I might need to warn you, but you seem to be fully cognisant of your situation. So... How can I help?"

"Why do you want to help me?" Dan asked, fear making him blunt.

The man shrugged. "You're actually part of a slightly larger picture here in Rome," he said mildly. "And, of course, you are my brother's namesake. He does seem to be indirectly responsible for some of your current problems."

Dan wasn't convinced. He didn't even know if this man was even really a priest. He could be anyone. He could be about to draw him into a trap.

"I'd like to hear the Hail Mary," he said.

The priest looked a little surprised. Dan said, doggedly, "If you're a priest, you'll know the Hail Mary. I'd like to hear you say it."

"Very well." The other man inclined his head. "In English, Italian, Latin or Greek?"

Dan wasn't going to be fobbed off. "English," he said.

He listened intently while the priest intoned, "Hail Mary,

full of grace, the Lord is with thee. Blessed art thou among women, and blessed is the fruit of thy womb, Jesus. Holy Mary, Mother of God, pray for us sinners, now and at the hour of our death. Amen."

A pause. The doorman made the sign of the cross. Dan, who had never been a Roman Catholic, decided that this meant it was probably correct. He looked into the hooded eyes of the priest, whose name he had forgotten.

"Now," the priest said. "Let's think about getting you out of here."

"There's someone waiting for me in the lobby," Dan said in a low voice. "Him and someone else – they've been following me all day. I can't... I can't go up to my room."

"Well, perhaps we could go in together," the priest said. "Sometimes it's best to be bold." And he tranquilly linked Dan's arm and led him in through the doors and over to the Reception Desk, where the clerk handed him the key to his suite. They continued over to the lifts, the priest keeping his body in its voluminous black coat between Dan and the nondescript young man. An assistant manager came over as the lift doors began to open.

"My dear Father Taylor," he said. "How very good to see you."

"Good evening, Enzo," the priest said. "It's very good to see you too. It seems no time at all since your wedding... Actually, I wonder if you could help us? My friend says that he's been having just a little trouble with his key. I wonder if someone could come up with us, just to make sure it's working?"

"That will be my pleasure, Father," the assistant manager responded, beaming. "My pleasure." And he got into the lift with them. A little more conversation about the wedding...

"Really? Two years ago already? How time flies..."

And they had arrived on his floor. Dan quickly scanned the corridor as they emerged. It looked empty, but there could easily be someone just around the corner, waiting. Maybe watching them in one of the corridor's mirrors. He felt ill with terror. He could almost feel the bullet as it struck him, severing his spinal cord. The second bullet would kill him.

The priest and the assistant manager found that the key was, in fact, working perfectly.

The assistant manager was about to leave them, but the priest said, "And, Enzo, if you wouldn't mind sparing us just one more minute of your time, my friend here has been just a little concerned about a flickering light in the bathroom."

"Of course," the assistant manager said. "Please allow me. Sometimes the bulbs we use don't last as long as they should. Let me check it for you, Mr Taylor."

He and the priest went ahead into the suite, and Dan followed them. The suite was empty. The bathroom light seemed to be functioning well, and, after casting a critical eye over the flowers in the vases and checking that the rooms had been perfectly dusted, the assistant manager beamed again, shook the priest's hand, bowed and left them. Dan grabbed his passport and wallet and shoved them into his pocket.

"Now," the priest said. "I suggest we take the back stairs, and find a quiet way out. Come this way, Mr Taylor."

The stairs had lights which came on as they were approached, so that the way ahead of them and the steps behind them were cast into darkness. Dan's ears strained for any sound that wasn't their feet, rapidly descending, and his eyes burned with the effort of peering ahead into blackness. They could be leapt upon at any moment. The man in the lobby must have seen them. Had probably followed them. Had no doubt texted his colleague.

Dan realised that he was drenched with sweat, and his breathing was as laboured as if he was climbing a mountain. Beside him, Father Taylor paused, briefly getting his bearings.

"Okay," he said. "This is the first floor. There's a service lift down to the laundry from this floor. I think if we just take a right turn through this door, and then a left turn, we'll be able to get there. And we should nicely avoid anyone who might be hoping to find us."

He steered Dan, who said, "How... How do you know all

this?"

Again, a slightly surprised glance.

"I took the precaution of studying the plans of the hotel before I came," the priest replied. "I thought it might be best for you to make a discreet exit, in the circumstances."

The lift stopped close to a noisy laundry room, swathed with sheets and tablecloths, where startled workers eyed them as they entered. The priest raised his hand in blessing, and briskly walked Dan past the washing machines and out through another door that led into storerooms and finally to a small back door which he unlatched. They were now outside, a moonlit sky above them, and close to the hotel's massive bins.

"I think," Father Taylor said, "that if we could just manage to get up on top, we'd be able to get over the wall without triggering the security lights. What do you think?"

Dan could only nod, and wonder if perhaps there really was a benign deity who had sent this strange person to rescue him. The priest cupped his hands, Dan placed his foot in them, and, with the boost up, managed just about to scramble onto the top of the bins. He then leant down, and grabbed the other man's hand, and, with more scrambling, the priest was on top with him. The wall was quite daunting. They could climb it, but it was the long drop on the other side that made Dan hesitate. But still, what was a broken ankle or two compared with a bullet in the spine? He climbed, he momentarily straddled the wall and hesitated, and then, eyes closed, he prepared himself and jumped.

He hit the ground hard, and lay for a couple of moments, winded. Father Taylor landed alongside him, and then got to his feet to brush his coat down.

"Okay?" he asked.

Dan nodded. He didn't seem to have broken anything.

"All right," the priest said approvingly. "Let's get you into a taxi and on your way to the airport. Where are you going to go?" he added, as they headed rapidly through the busy evening to a taxi rank.

"I'm not sure," Dan said. "My friend thought I should go

and stay with my brother…"

"Where does he live?"

"Boston. Massachusetts."

"That sounds like a good idea," the priest said. They had arrived at the rows of taxis outside Termini. He shook Dan's hand.

Dan said, "I don't know how to thank you…" and Father Taylor smiled and waved his thanks away.

"I'm just sorry you've been through such an unpleasant experience," he said. "You've been very brave. Good luck with the rest of your journey."

He closed the taxi door with a wave. Dan turned to watch his tall figure striding away as his taxi began to weave through the traffic and out to the airport at Fiumicino. He still couldn't quite shake off the feeling that he was being followed….but that was ridiculous. He'd made it. He was on his way.

Chapter Forty-Five

"He thought he could go without me," Sophia explained, as they sat with coffee at the airport. Julian smiled. Daniel sighed.

"It's just that this is probably a complete wild goose chase," he said. "As this whole job has been."

"Well, frankly, I'll be glad to see you out of Rome," his brother said. "The tourist managed it, and I think it will simplify things when you've gone as well."

Daniel could only agree. The police had arrived shortly after the shooting stopped, and in the hours after dawn had searched the gardens, while the detective sat in the kitchen with the family and Daniel. He too, had seemed to think it was a good idea for Daniel to leave the city.

"We can call you back if we need you to give evidence at a later date," he said. "But... Frankly, I don't know if we're going to manage any arrests any time soon." He held up a hand to stop Alessandro speaking. "Yes, I know you're sure that Silvestri's behind this, but proving it could be extremely difficult. And it could be someone else, with quite a different agenda. We just don't know yet. Enquiries are continuing."

Alessandro just muttered. Livia embraced Daniel.

"You look after yourself," she said. "Be careful, Daniel. Don't get shot again." And Agnese kissed him on the cheek with her soft lips.

She said, "If it wasn't for my lovely Julio..." and smiled.

Chapter Forty-Six

"Dan! Dan!"

This was Gloria, Sam's wife, model-like in jeans and jumper and long black hair, leaning over the rail as he entered Arrivals at Boston airport, beaming.

"Good to see you," she said, giving him a peck on each cheek. "Sam's in the car – parking's a nightmare here. Did you have a good flight?"

Dan nodded, and allowed himself to be bustled outside, to where Sam was waiting, and then bundled into the back seat. It was only then that he noticed the large, burnished, golden dog that lay in the footwell, waving a lazy tail at him. Sam grinned at him through the mirror.

"Good to see you, bro," he said, as he accelerated into rivers of traffic. "And I don't think you've met Cicero before. He's Gloria's dog, and now he's ours."

Dan leaned forward and patted the dog's head.

"Thanks for this," he said.

"No problem. We're having quite a busy time with visitors," Sam said. Unlike Dan, he liked people, unexpected events, social occasions. He'd enjoyed his wedding. And Gloria was just the same.

"You're going to be in the games room," she said. "It's got an incredibly comfortable pull-out bed. And you'll have to tell us all about your adventures. Rome sounds amazing."

Dan nodded again. In their company, he felt lumpy, ungracious, sour. He wanted to rise to an appropriate level of animation and friendliness, but he wasn't sure he had it in him. He was still aching all over. More than anything, he was tired. He felt that he could lie down on the incredibly comfortable pull-out bed and sleep forever.

He said, "I've taken some great pictures."

"We'd love to see them," Gloria said. "It's incredible that we've never been there… We got as far as Florence, but that was it. We never got to Rome."

"So we need to see your photos," Sam said cheerfully, while driving with what seemed to Dan quite astonishing confidence. Dan just nodded, dourly.

They lived in Cambridge, in a generous clapboard New England house on a tree-lined street. Spring hadn't yet arrived – the buds on the branches were tightly furled, the sky a pale, wintry blue.

"Coffee," Gloria said decisively, showing Dan into their warm kitchen. Dan watched her as she filled the cafetière, and put what looked like home-made cookies onto a plate. Sam came in from parking the car, and kissed her. Dan looked away.

Sam said, "I'll go and see if our other visitor is awake yet. He might want coffee."

As he went out, Gloria said, in a low, confiding voice, "He's a friend of Sam's – they met at a conference, and they both work in the same field… But since he's been here, he's been a bit weird, to be honest…"

And it was at approximately that moment that Dan's world stopped.

Gloria may have said something more, and probably did, but Dan's eyes were fixed on the Italian who had just walked in. His dark eyes met Dan's, acknowledged him, and, when Sam introduced them, he reached over and shook Dan's hand with a smile.

"Sabato," he said.

Dan said, "Good to meet you again," and put his coffee cup down in case he spilt it.

"I don't know if you guys got much of a chance to talk at the wedding," Sam said. "Those things are always so busy. But this, Sabato, is my brother, fresh from Rome."

"Ciao," Dan said, and then immediately hated himself.

But Sabato smiled, the slowest and sexiest smile that Dan had ever seen, and said, "I think you've picked up a Rome accent."

Sam and Gloria were busy organising the kitchen table.

"Dinner in half an hour," Gloria said. "Why don't you two go into the living room while we get things moving in here? We're going to try out our organic stuffed peppers with sweet potato." She took the coffee pot and plate of cookies into the bright, assured living room and put them down on a low table. Dan sat down on a sofa, and Sabato also sat down. Quite a way away from him, but on the same sofa.

"More coffee?" Dan asked, but Sabato shook his head with a smile of thanks. Dan topped up his own cup, and took a cookie, just for something to do. Naturally, now that he was in the presence of the most beautiful man in the world, he couldn't think of anything to say. Nothing. He chomped his cookie.

Sabato said, "I might go outside and have a smoke…"

Dan nodded. "Me too."

Sabato said, "Really? You smoke?"

And Dan had to say, "No, I don't actually… smoke. But I'd be glad of some fresh air."

Sabato smiled and shrugged. But it was a good-natured smile, and Dan determinedly followed him out onto the deck, where there was a set of wrought-iron chairs, a table and an ashtray.

"I should stop," Sabato said, rolling a thin cigarette. "When all this is over, I'm going to stop."

"All what?" Dan asked.

Sabato frowned. "I got mixed up in something scary," he said. "I'm just waiting for my friend to come, and then it should finally be sorted out. For me, anyway."

Of course there was a friend.

Dan said, "Is your friend Italian?"

And Sabato looked at him, laughed with dawning understanding, and said, "No, he's an English guy. Not that there's anything wrong with being English. But we're not… you know, close. He's just a guy."

They sat on the heavy chairs, Sabato smoking, Dan watching him. He would have happily stayed there forever.

Then Gloria called, "Come and get it, guys!" and they

went in to dinner.

There were candles on the table, and platters of food, and wine glasses.

Sam said, "I can't remember the last time we ate together like this, Dan – it must have been when I came to see you in London."

Dan could barely remember that visit, except for the sense of chewed-up resentment that Sam's cheerful, American-white smile had provoked. He felt ashamed. His brother was, actually, a good and generous man, and he needed to just get over it. He also, he knew, needed to get over Sabato. There was no way. None at all.

And so they ate, and chatted, and Dan made an effort to relax. He consciously drank a couple of large glasses of red wine, and felt the tension in his shoulders slowly dissolving. A third glass seemed like a good idea, and he had already poured this, and taken a sip, when Sabato's phone gave its little alert and Dan saw his face change colour.

And then the doorbell rang.

"Don't..." he said, but Gloria had already risen, and he could hear the door opening, and voices, and he turned his head slowly as she came back into the kitchen. Behind her, Mario. Whip-thin, cold-eyed, his mouth curved into some sort of smile that Sam and Gloria seemed to mistake for the real thing. Sam was on his feet, surprised, but in a pleased way. He offered Mario a seat, a glass, a plate.

Dan felt as if things had started to move in slow motion. And he could see that Sabato felt the same way – he seemed hypnotised by Mario's presence, and had put his fork down absently, as though he had forgotten the reason why he was holding it.

"Che sorpresa, Sabato," Mario said. "Come stai?"

From his basket in the corner, Cicero growled.

"Bene, Mario," Sabato said softly.

"So you two know each other," Mario added, his eyes shifting speculatively from Sabato to Dan.

"This is turning into a Roman reunion," Sam said, opening another bottle of wine. "What brings you to this side of the pond, Mario?"

"The same thing that has brought Sabato," Mario replied, matching Sam's good-humoured tone, accepting a glass of red wine, casting his chill smile around the table. "And Dan, of course."

"Really?" Sam topped up glasses and smiled, expecting the conversation to continue. But there was just a growing silence.

Then Mario said, "Yes, really.' He swilled the untasted wine around in his glass. "This is what I think we call the end-game."

The wine Dan had drunk had abruptly faded. He knew he should intervene in some way, but couldn't think how to.

Meanwhile, Sam said, "I'm sorry, I don't quite understand…"

Mario said, "It doesn't matter whether you understand or not, Doctor Taylor." He stood up.

"It's over, little man," he said to Sabato. "The whole thing is over. You have no protection and nowhere left to go. I'm going to give you an hour to hand the ring to me." He put the wine glass down. "I have American colleagues outside. We're waiting. One hour."

Dan thought, slowly and clearly, He's completely serious. He's probably armed. He's in my brother's house. He has followed me here, and this is therefore my fault.

He said, "Mario, none of this has anything to do with my family."

Mario glanced at him briefly. "No, you're right. It has nothing to do with you, either. But that hasn't stopped you getting involved with Silvestri and his dogs, has it, Dan?" He spoke his name with contempt, and said, "I'll see myself out." The front door slammed behind him.

Sabato said, "I'm sorry. I'm really sorry. I'm in trouble, and it was a mistake for me to come here. I need to go…"

At that moment the doorbell rang again.

Chapter Forty-Seven

Whatever Daniel had been expecting, it hadn't been this – an abandoned dinner table, a bewildered couple, a stressed and blinking English relative, a barking dog, and Sabato, more nervous than ever. He briefly shook hands with the couple and introduced Sophia, while Sabato waited with visible impatience, and then grabbed Daniel by the arm and hurried him out of the kitchen and into his guest room.

He said, "Mario is here, he's just been here."

Daniel frowned. "How did he find you?"

"I think he followed the Englishman. Sam's brother." Sabato pulled his backpack down from the top of the wardrobe. "He's given me an hour to give him the ring. I don't know how we're going to get out..." He delved into one of the bag's pockets.

Daniel began to say, "And how did you think I could help...?" and then his voice trailed off as he looked at what Sabato was holding in the palm of his hand. For once he was lost for words.

"That's... it," he said finally. "The ring."

And Sabato nodded sombrely. "I only found it by accident."

He showed Daniel the zipped inside pouch where Francesco had put it. "He must have been short of time," Sabato said. "He must have known that Mario was coming for him. He just... hid it."

Daniel took the ring and examined it carefully. The striped stone was worn, uneven and faintly rippled, the lion's head at its centre still sharply cut. There was no doubt that this was the real thing. He looked up at Sabato.

"And now?"

Sabato shook his head. "I don't know. Mario thinks I

know where it is, and that's why he hasn't killed me. Once he's got it, he will kill me. And maybe the others as well." He felt in his pocket for a cigarette. "I don't know what to do. I don't know how to get us all out of this."

Seemingly for the first time, he noticed Daniel's crutch, and his bruised face.

"Daniel – what happened?"

Daniel shook his head. "It doesn't matter."

And then, before he could say more, there was the sound of the doorbell, and Gloria's voice, raised, saying "You can't just walk in here," and then a voice that he recognised.

He came out of Sabato's room, and saw that the doorway was filled with the bulk of the Russian, who said, "You see? My friend is here. Daniel. Daniel, who is this woman?"

"You know this man?" Gloria said uncertainly to Daniel. And the Russian took advantage of her momentary hesitation to advance into the hallway and embrace him.

"Do I know him?" the Russian repeated, shaking his head. "I have never known anyone so difficult to stay in touch with." He wagged a large finger. "He doesn't listen to Sophia, who is his security, he doesn't tell me what he knows, even though I'm his client..." He continued to talk, his arm around Daniel's shoulders, as they made their way back into the kitchen. There, he nodded amiably at the others and sat down. He made the spacious room seem small.

He shook hands with Sophia. He peered at the English visitor. "Have I seen you before, somewhere....?"

But the man shook his head emphatically.

The Russian shrugged, and then said, "I have some men outside. One of them has some gifts for you – can I invite him in?"

Sam and Gloria exchanged a look, and then Sam said, "I... suppose so."

The Russian used his phone, and a gaunt man wearing a fedora and a black overcoat came in, his arms around a large basket. He put it down on the table and silently withdrew.

"See," the Russian said, delving into the basket. "Caviar, the best in the world. And vodka, and champagne. What else would a Russian bring you? Where's your fridge...?" He rummaged around, looking for ice.

"Who... Who exactly is this?" Sam asked Daniel.

"He's been looking for the ring of Diocletian," Daniel said. "He employed me and Sophia..."

"So he's the Russian," the English relative said, looking a little dazed. "He's..."

At that moment the Russian returned with ice and glasses.

"Please," he said. "Everybody, take a small drink with me. It's a courtesy. Please, Gloria, here. And you, Sophia." He beamed and handed round vodka. "You're friends of Daniel's, and that means you're friends of mine too."

Sam said, "I'm sorry, but I don't..."

"No, of course," the Russian said, almost contritely, sitting back with his glass. "You're having a wonderful evening here, I can see that, and I'm interrupting it." He looked at the Englishman, and then at Sam. "Are you two related? You could be."

He sipped his drink. "Daniel here has been on a quest for me, and he got himself shot in Rome – even though I warned him about Rome, and even though Sophia here was looking out for him – and now he's here. And it looks like he's whacked his head. I don't understand it, that's all. I ask him for reports, and I don't get them." He turned to Sam. "I've had two experts now. One of them wrote me long, long reports that said nothing, and now this one doesn't write me anything at all. What would you do?"

He shrugged, expansively and good-humouredly. "I give him a secure phone to use, and he doesn't use it. So... I decided to fly over and see what my expert was up to. Maybe he's got good news for me, I thought..." He smiled, to show that he was being jocular, but he looked enquiringly at Daniel.

Daniel cleared his throat. Really, at this point, he was uncertain. He looked towards Sabato, but Sabato simply looked terrified. The Russian's phone rang, and he spoke briefly and put it back on the table.

"Well," Daniel said, "there's been a development. An

interesting development..."

Sabato said, "I'm... just going to the bathroom."

"He's going outside to smoke," the Russian said dismissively, following him with his eyes as he left the room. "Nicotine addiction is a terrible thing. He needs to be careful." He looked reproachfully at Sam. "This is a rough area," he said. "An area where fascists seem to congregate. Fortunately we have protection."

Sam said, "I think we need to call the police."

"I'm sure that's not necessary," the Russian said blandly. "I'm sure we can wrap up our business and leave you and your charming family in peace." He beamed at Gloria. "American women are so beautiful," he said. "Glamorous. They have glamour." He turned to Daniel. "You were saying that there's been a development...?"

Daniel hesitated, but there was no sign of Sabato. And so he opened his hand.

The Russian caught his breath, and then lifted the ring slowly, turning it in the light, his eyes shining.

"What a beautiful thing," he said softly. "What a magnificent thing." He eased it gently onto his ring finger. "Look at that. Just look. It fits." He took it off again and put it reverently down on the table.

Daniel said, "It was Sabato who found it, not me. You'll have to negotiate the price with him."

The oligarch gave a derisive snort. "He should be grateful he isn't dead."

It was then that Sophia said, "Where is Sabato?"

The Englishman said, "I'll go and look for him. Maybe he isn't well..."

But the bathroom was empty. Sabato was no longer in the house.

The Russian stood up. "So he's run away," he said. "So what. Daniel, you'll have your fee tomorrow." He fastened up his coat in preparation for the New England evening outside.

Sophia said to him, "No. You need to wait. There's a problem here."

"Not my problem," the Russian said.

And then Daniel's phone rang.

"We have him." Mario's voice, as clear as if he was in the room. "It's a simple exchange. The ring, or else we leave his corpse on the steps. And then we'll kill the rest of you, one by one."

The Russian shook his head. "Pathetic threats," he said. "Relax. I have ten men outside, all competent, all armed. They'll deal with these fascists, if that's what you want. There's only six of them, in a van. I despise fascists."

Sophia said, "I'm sorry, but I don't think we have a choice. We need to get the hostage back."

The Russian shook his head. "Absolutely not," he said. "Our business is concluded."

Sophia drew her gun. "I must insist," she said.

The lights went out.

Sam swore, and Gloria fell over the Russian while trying to get round him. She found candles in a cupboard and lit them. The dog howled.

"For God's sake – there's a gun pointing at you," the Englishman shouted at the Russian. "Give us the ring now."

The Russian lifted one of the candles which Gloria had lit. The light flickered across his face, so that his eyes shone in the dark caverns of his sockets.

"No-one is going to shoot me, you dog," he said to the overwrought Englishman. "Shut your stupid mouth." He glanced at Sophia. "Do you think I have no self-respect? Is that what you think? If I gave way to trash like those fascists, I wouldn't be worthy of the ring. It stays here." It was in front of him on the table. "It's mine, you know that. My men will do all they can to avoid casualties. Now put that gun away. You look ridiculous."

And Sophia hesitated, her finger on the safety catch.

It was then that the Englishman grabbed the ring.

Chapter Forty-Eight

His rage had been sudden, and had swept through him like a cleansing forest fire.

The Russian couldn't be threatened, couldn't be reasoned with. No point in trying to find middle ground. Sabato was close to death, and the Russian was just going to walk away. The ring was heavier than he had expected: it weighted his fist in a satisfying way as he made it onto the street. He could see the fascists' van, parked under a tree, and two of the Russian's men crouched behind parked cars on the opposite side of the road. He ran, bent low, zigzagging. He could feel his heart thumping in his throat, and he tripped over a tree root and almost fell, but he lurched on, while behind him he began to hear gunfire, and guessed that they were shooting at him. Again, he imagined the bullet that would hit him, a sudden white-hot agony that would fell him, but he grasped the ring tighter and ran faster. He knew where he was going and he knew what he was going to do.

He felt like the last runner in a relay race, with everything resting on his speed. People were running after him now, there was more gunfire, but he couldn't look behind him. He could only speed up, hurtling through the evening, flinging himself across roads and around corners until finally there it was. The bridge across the River Charles.

Dan didn't pause. He raced across the bridge, dodging traffic, almost colliding with a runner wearing earphones, and scrambled up onto the wide stone parapet. How did he feel? Joyful. He stretched out his arm so that the hand holding the ring was over the water. He put out his other arm to steady himself.

He could see figures appearing out of the darkness; he could see Mario's white, livid face.

"Stay back," he shouted. "Shoot me and the ring goes in the river."

Now he could see his brother, and Gloria, and the Italian woman, and the lumbering figure of the Russian.

"You want the ring, you bring Sabato here," he yelled. "Bring him to me."

A couple of shots were fired. He felt a fierce hiss as a bullet howled past his face.

"The ring will go into the river," he yelled again, warningly. His knuckles around it were white. He had never felt so free or so powerful. "Bring Sabato here," he yelled again. "Bring him now, or you lose the ring."

There was a long pause. There were people congregated at both ends of the bridge. His brother tried to edge forward, saying, "Dan, please, this is madness..."

But he shouted, "Stay back, Sam. Don't come near me. Tell them to bring Sabato."

Mario was shouting something, but Dan didn't even try to listen.

"Bring Sabato," he yelled back. "Or I throw the ring." And he mimed a throwing gesture for emphasis.

And then he could see two men dragging Sabato onto the bridge. He was still alive.

"Let him go," Dan yelled. "Let him come to me and I'll come down. Let him walk to me."

Another pause. The men holding Sabato let go of him, shoved him towards Dan. Dan waited. Sabato moved forward uncertainly and reluctantly. His face was rigid with fear. He raised his eyes to Dan.

Dan whispered, "When I count three, Sabato – jump into the river. Trust me."

He looked into Sabato's eyes. The Italian gave a slow nod of understanding. From far away they could hear sirens approaching.

"One... two..." Dan whispered, as he buttoned the ring into his pocket...

"Three!" he shouted, and pitched himself off the bridge and into the swift black waters below.

Chapter Forty-Nine

"Catch them and shoot them."

"You can't just—"

But the Russian was walking away, breathing heavily, pale with wrath.

Chapter Fifty

The water hit him with a force that took his breath away. He went under, kicked out wildly, flailed, went under again, and briefly surfaced. He saw the lights of the shore shifting from horizontal to vertical, and then he was underwater again, in darkness, struggling helplessly. He felt a hand seizing his shirt, pulling him up to the surface, and then he saw Sabato's face close to him.

"Swim," Sabato said. "I've got you."

The bridge was now some distance away, and they were in the broad reaches of the river, with the lights of the city far away. He could also see lights on the surface of the water, moving. He was so cold that he could barely move, but he kicked out his legs, and moved his arms in time with Sabato, who was steering them towards a large clump of trees which stood around a long curve of the river, at the edge of the water. Dan lost track of time as they fought their way towards them, and he had swallowed a lot more water before they were finally able to haul themselves onto the shingle. They lay, hidden by low-hanging branches, sodden and exhausted and shivering uncontrollably.

Finally Dan said, "We have to get to shelter. We can't stay here." He sat up, and tried to get his bearings. He checked his shirt. As well as the ring, he still had his credit card and his sodden passport buttoned into his breast pocket.

"Let's see if we can get onto a train," he said.

Boston's cathedral-like main station, lined with giant advertisements for Dolce & Gabbana, was still busy, but not crowded, in the late evening. Dan knew how conspicuous they looked, squelching in their sodden shoes, their clothes clinging to them, their hair dripping. They scanned the Departure boards.

"New York?" Dan asked, and Sabato just nodded. While they waited, they cleaned themselves up in the toilets, using the hand dryers to dry themselves a little. "I can't believe we've made it here," Sabato said.

For the first time since his mad run, Dan smiled.

"We're here, and we've got the ring," he said.

Chapter Fifty-One

"What did he say?"

"He just said they're both okay. He was calling from a public phone."

Sam switched his phone off. It was midnight. The power line which the fascists had cut was still down, and so they sat by candlelight around the kitchen table – he, Gloria, Sophia, and Daniel. The men in the van had melted into the night once the police car appeared at the end of the bridge, and the Russian had also retreated, still barking orders into his phone.

"He doesn't say where they are?" Daniel asked.

Sam shook his head. "I'm amazed he didn't drown," he said. "He was never much of a swimmer."

He rubbed his hands over his face. "I guess we should all try to get some sleep." He and Gloria had made up beds for Daniel and Sophia. "I hope you'll be comfortable," he said. "I hope you've got enough bedding… I know it's a lot colder here than in Rome…"

"I'm sure we'll be fine," Sophia said. "Thank you."

As they rose from the table Daniel's phone rang, and he saw that it was the Russian. He hesitated, and then answered it cautiously.

"Daniel, we need to talk."

"Okay. Perhaps we can talk tomorrow."

"No, Daniel – it has to be now."

A silence.

"Daniel? Are you there?"

"Yes."

"I don't blame you for what's happened, Daniel. You did find the ring. It wasn't your fault that little bastard ran off with it."

Another silence.

"And I don't really blame Sophia. She panicked. It was a tense situation. Although she shouldn't have pointed her gun at me. But she was under stress, I understand that."

"Okay…"

"So now we just need to find them."

"We?"

"I need someone with some expertise," the Russian said. "The men I brought over here haven't acquitted themselves well. In fact they're morons. I need you, Daniel. To find Sabato and bring the ring back to me."

Daniel said, "I really don't think…"

"Okay," the Russian said. "We'll talk tomorrow. It's late now. Sleep on it, Daniel."

Daniel sighed and put his phone away.

Chapter Fifty-Two

Dan and Sabato sat in the splendour of Grand Central Station and sipped coffee.

"Do you think anyone's followed us?" Sabato asked.

"I don't know." The fear which had dogged Dan since Rome was back. He was now no longer sure whether the ring was a bargaining chip or a death sentence. He had no idea what they should do.

Sabato said, "I wish I had my phone."

Dan tried to think. He said, "I can get cash on my card. We need to buy clothes. And flights…"

"Flights where?"

And Dan didn't know. Rome seemed impossible, and so did London. Where could they go that was out of the global reach of both Silvestri and the Russian?

But meanwhile they went shopping for practical, anonymous American clothes – jeans, zipped jackets, baseball caps. Sabato drew the line at cheap trainers.

"I'm sorry, Dan, but I have to have decent shoes. I just have to."

From there, they went to a random, small hotel where they took turns to shower and shave. Then they bought burgers and fries in a bright, downtown diner.

"You look quite American," Sabato said, as they ate.

Dan smiled. "So do you," he said. For a moment he felt encouraged, but the feeling ebbed again. "But we can't stay here – we're too easy to find."

They finished their meal in sombre silence. Then Sabato said, "I have an idea."

Chapter Fifty-Three

Julian had called him early in the morning.

"Daniel, I wonder if we could have a word..." He was unusually hesitant. "There's something you probably don't know, and this is possibly a good time..."

Daniel waited.

"In fact, it's definitely a good time."

He could hear his brother taking a breath.

"I've learnt quite a lot about the Roman ring you've been looking for," he added. "It's the ring of St Sebastian, blessed with the saint's blood. It's something that the church would very much like to recover. And if the church reclaimed it, it would, in effect, put it beyond dispute. In fact..." Another pause.

"In fact?"

"In fact, it seems that Sophia has just been retained by us to do just that."

Daniel just blinked. "What...?"

"It seems that the relevant people in the Vatican have made contact with her because of her links with the Russian, and her undoubted ability."

"But..." He didn't bother to say Are you sure? Because Julian was always sure.

Julian said, "This is all confidential, of course, Daniel..." He paused again. "And they would very much like to retain you as well, if they could."

Daniel said, "I don't think so, Julian."

He didn't answer the Russian when he called. He had booked a taxi to take him to the airport. Sophia, back from her early morning run, noticed his bag in the hallway, and looked at him enquiringly.

He said, "I'm heading back to London." Adding, rather

more sourly than he had intended, "I'm afraid you're on your own now."

"I don't understand, Daniel."

"You've got a new client."

"Oh." Sophia sat down. "Yes, I was going to talk to you about that." She began to unlace her trainers. "I wouldn't have agreed, of course, but after last night I was so pissed off with the Russian…" She looked at him. "You could help," she said. "But… Maybe you've had enough."

"I've done my job," he said, feeling himself stubborn and sullen and graceless. "I'm not responsible for what happens next."

Sophia nodded. "That's true, you're not." She glanced at him again, and put on a pot of coffee. Daniel, bag in hand, was somehow still there.

"I've been thinking about it," she said. "Sabato's passport is here. That means they can't legally leave the States. So we could start by checking trains and Greyhound buses. What do you think?"

Daniel hesitated. He might regret this. But…

Chapter Fifty-Four

The radio was playing and Sabato was driving, a cigarette drooping from his hand, scenery flashing past the open window. Dan lounged in the passenger seat. How could he have ever dreamed of this? America streamed past them, and Sabato hummed along to the country songs that crackled from the car's speakers.

They had been travelling for four days, driving in six-hour shifts, stopping overnight at ramshackle motels. They had lived mostly on cans of soda and potato chips that they kept stacked in the footwell, and all the time they were heading west.

"Amazing country," Sabato said, glancing at Dan from behind his sunglasses. Dan nodded.

Sabato said, "You know, I still can't get over what you did. You saved my life."

"And you saved mine," Dan said. "I'd have drowned in the river."

Sabato nodded slowly and thoughtfully, gunning the car down the long, empty road.

"Pretty cool, huh?" he said.

Dan nodded again. It didn't matter that Sabato was way out of his league. It just didn't matter. He was content to simply be in his company, swinging west, with a wide blue sky above them. In fact, it was more than he would ever have hoped for.

"Sam's a great guy," Sabato said. "He and Gloria have been so kind to me. You're lucky to have him for a brother."

And Dan said, "Yes, I know I am," and managed a smile.

"Sam talked about you," Sabato continued, his eyes on the road ahead of them. "He said you'd always been a great big brother."

Dan looked at him. Was he being sarcastic?

"He said he was bullied by a kid at school when he was about seven, and you were about ten. This was a very malevolent kid. He said it had made his life a misery, and he'd started to be terrified of going to school. You stopped it, just by talking to the kid. You explained to him that Sam was your brother, and the kid had to leave him alone."

Dan had some faint, residual memory of a solid child with hard blue eyes... Not entirely dissimilar to Mario, in fact.

"He said that was typical of you," Sabato said. "Even at ten years old, you understood people. And you helped, and that's what you still do."

Dan felt pleased, in a perplexed kind of way. It was as though Sam had been talking about someone else. Someone who bore a faint resemblance to him, but wasn't him.

Finally, as they drove alongside tall, dark fir forests, they saw a sign: Aberdeen 30 miles. And Sabato smiled.

"Nearly there," he said.

Chapter Fifty-Five

"Nothing." Sophia switched her laptop off. She rubbed her eyes. "This is like… There's a saying in English…"

"A needle in a haystack," Daniel said.

Sophia nodded. "That's what this is like. Two guys, a whole country…" She drummed her fingernails against the keyboard. "By the time we find their trail, they could have sold the ring, bought passports… They could be anywhere." She leaned back. "Maybe you were right. Maybe I just need to hand this back to the Vatican, and they can hire an agency over here." She sighed. "I hate letting things go."

Daniel had been looking at a large map of the USA. The idea he'd had from the night Sabato vanished into the river was still there.

He said. "I think I might know where they've gone."

Chapter Fifty-Six

As they approached the house, Sabato slowed gently.

"What kind of car do your friends have?" Dan asked.

"A pickup truck, I think," Sabato said. They looked at the dark green Toyota that was parked outside the front gate.

"Maybe they have visitors," Sabato added.

"Maybe," Dan agreed. He glanced at the Italian. "No-one knew we were coming here?"

Sabato shook his head, and switched the engine off. "What do we do?" he asked.

As if Dan knew. He said, "Maybe we wait."

Sabato nodded. "Okay."

They sat on, while the bright, clear afternoon sky began to slowly change colour, and distant birds spiralled down from the sky to roost on faraway trees. They were down to their last can of soda. A middle-aged man over the road, who had been occasionally peering at them through the window, now came out onto his porch. He had a watering can, and he scattered water onto his plant pots and openly studied them.

"He looks like he might call the police," Sabato said. He looked again at the green car. "If they're visitors, they're staying a very long time."

"It can't be anyone who knows us," Dan said.

"Maybe one of us should knock on the door."

"Maybe." He looked at Sabato. "You know them."

"You could keep the engine running," Sabato said. "And leave my door open."

"Okay."

Sabato got out of the car. Dan shifted into the driving seat and switched the engine on. He leaned over and opened the passenger door. Sabato looked at the house for a moment. He took a deep breath. And then he walked towards it.

Chapter Fifty-Seven

They had spent the afternoon looking at Eric's photographs and drinking strong tea. Jeanette had also found some English muffins buried deep in her freezer, and at four o'clock she ceremoniously served these, defrosted, with butter and jam.

"English people love these," she explained to Sophia. "Try one – they're not bad."

"Thank you," Sophia said. Her cup of brown, milky tea was slowly going cold beside her.

Eric said, "It's going to be dark soon. Are you folks going to stay for dinner?"

"No," Sophia said quickly. "Thank you very much, but we've put you to enough trouble."

"It's no problem," Jeanette said. "I've got a recipe for shepherd's pie – it's a traditional British dish. I make it with instant mashed potato, to give it a really nice texture, and it's pretty quick."

"Really," Sophia said. "We'll... Maybe we'll call back tomorrow, if that's possible?"

"You'd be very welcome," Eric said. "But I do wonder if that Italian boy is going to show up again."

Chapter Fifty-Eight

Dan watched Sabato knock on the door. He saw a woman wearing slacks and a blue blouse open the door, and laugh, and usher him into the house. This all looked quite positive. The ring was in the glove compartment. It was wrapped in cotton wool, and wedged into an empty cigarette packet. He sipped on the last of the soda, aware of the middle-aged man's gaze becoming more intent. He did, he had to acknowledge, now look quite suspicious. He wondered if he could close the car door.

And then Sabato came out of the house again. He was nodding.

"It's okay, Dan. It's my friend Daniel."

Dan hesitated. "Doesn't he work for the Russian?"

Sabato said, "It's okay. Really. Bring the ring in."

Again Dan hesitated. "Sabato, after all we've been through…"

And then the unthinkable happened. Sabato leaned down through the car window and kissed him on the lips. Over the road, the middle-aged man's eyes widened.

"After all we've been through," Sabato said, "you can trust me, Dan."

Chapter Fifty-Nine

"There," Jeanette said. "It isn't often we have company. Especially not British company." She dished up portions of shepherd's pie onto pale green plates, and topped them off with boiled carrots. "You must all be hungry, after all this travelling."

Dan loved shepherd's pie. He accepted the bottle of ketchup, and squirted a small pool onto the side of his plate, for dipping purposes. He noticed that Sabato wasn't actually eating very much, and neither was Sophia, the red-haired woman. Daniel, the thin guy, had declined, and was just drinking a cup of Jeanette's strong tea.

"This is fantastic," he told Jeanette. Eric, too, ate with relish.

After dinner, they retired to the sitting room.

"Well, this is certainly something," Eric said, picking up the ring again. It lay on its cotton wool bed on the mantelpiece. "I'm glad you brought it so we could see it... That was very thoughtful of you. I bet it could tell some tales."

Dan would have relaxed, just a little, but now a huge, huge new question was humming in his head. Sabato had kissed him. Sabato. Had. Kissed. Him.

"I'm sorry?" he said, as Jeanette spoke to him. "Oh, more tea? Yes, that would be great. Thank you."

And then there was a knock on the door.

"It's okay," Jeanette said, as Dan and Sabato rose. "That will just be my neighbour, Sybil. She usually calls in around now."

"Are you sure?" Sophia asked. "Shall I come with you...?" But Jeanette shook her head reassuringly, and went out into the hall.

Then the screen door crashed open, and the Russian, scowling and dusty, appeared in the doorway. He ignored Jeanette, and everyone else, and glared at Daniel.

"So," he said. "What is this nonsense I've had from this priest brother of yours? The Vatican owns the ring? Since when? Since when?"

He loomed, huge and furious. "You think I've got time to drive half way across America to this arsehole of a place? Is that what you think?" The gun he held shone darkly in the living room lights.

"I'll take the ring now," he said. "You've broken your contract with me, Daniel, and that's serious. You can be grateful I haven't just shot you – it's what you deserve. You too, Sophia. I expected better of you. Much better. You put your trust in people, and they turn out to be crooks..." Muttering, he reached over to take the ring from the mantelpiece.

Eric said, "I'd advise you to back off, Ruskie," and Dan saw that he had reached down to the side of his chair and scooped up the shotgun that lay there. Its barrel was now poking into the Russian's wide belly.

"And drop your gun," Eric added. "Pick it up," he instructed Sabato. "Hands over your head," he added.

The Russian stepped back, his hands raised, his face working speechlessly.

"Want me to plug him?" he asked Daniel casually. "My eyesight isn't what it was, but he's big enough. I'd hit something."

Daniel shook his head. "Tell him to sit down," he said.

"Sit down," Eric rapped.

The Russian subsided onto a chair.

"This isn't the end," he said. "You think this is over?"

Eric said, "I think I should just plug him. He isn't listening."

The Russian muttered something.

Jeanette said, "I've called the police. They'll be here in fifteen minutes or so. They have to come from the other side of town."

The Russian said, "You can't do this. I have a plane waiting…"

"Guess you better cancel it," Eric said. "You're going to be spending tonight in Aberdeen police cells. And probably a lot of nights after that. It's going to take them some time to figure out what to do with you."

The Russian said, "Daniel, this is ridiculous. You know me. You're not really going to let this happen?"

Eric said, "What do you think, Daniel? Think that if we maybe knew he was going to just get on his plane and go home…?"

Daniel shrugged.

"Come on, Daniel," the Russian said. He glanced warily at Eric. "I have a cramp. I can stand up?"

"What do you think, Daniel? Are we going to let him stand up?"

Daniel nodded slowly. "He can stand up."

The Russian rose. "I want to get on my plane."

Eric glanced enquiringly at Daniel, who hesitated.

"Come on, Daniel," the Russian said, glancing at his watch. "We haven't got all night."

"How long until the police arrive?" Daniel asked Jeanette.

"Ten minutes," she said. "Maybe five."

"Daniel, I need to get on my plane. I can't be arrested in America. It will humiliate me."

Daniel considered.

Eric said, "I don't figure you'll get bail – you're a flight risk."

"Jesus, Daniel. We need to just resolve this. Amicably."

Daniel sat back.

"And quickly," the Russian said.

A minute ticked by.

"Come on," the Russian said.

Another minute.

"What do you think?" Eric asked. "Guess we're running out of time…"

"Daniel," the Russian said. "I have to go. Please."

Daniel allowed another minute to pass. Then he said,

"Okay."

"Okay," the Russian repeated, his eyes still fixed uneasily on Eric and his gun. "Don't let the mad old man shoot me."

They watched him as he backed out of the house and then shovelled himself into his waiting taxi.

Eric grinned. "Well, this has been a night," he said, as he lowered the shotgun onto the floor again. "One day I'm going to have to get some ammunition for this thing."

Chapter Sixty

"So you've got your passport?"

"Of course I've got my passport, Julian."

They were in his rooms in Rome, the walls decorated only with a crucifix, but with a view of stone angels through the high windows. Julian shrugged mildly.

"It's worth asking. You remember the time you forgot it?"

Daniel smiled. "That was a very long time ago."

He glanced down at the text message which had just arrived. "It's Livia. They're pleased with the offer the Vatican has made... Pleased and a bit surprised." He looked at his brother. "How did you persuade the Church to buy back its own property?"

Julian shrugged modestly. "I gave it a little thought, and took a little advice," he replied. "It seems that the Church voluntarily gave the ring to Il Duce as a gift when he became Emperor. Perhaps not a wholehearted gift, but an expedient one. And since his descendants are gracious enough to be willing to return it to us, there clearly should be some recompense. We would want to do what was morally right, after all." He tranquilly drained his coffee cup.

It was time to say goodbye.

"You've done a good job, Daniel," Julian said,

Daniel smiled. He hadn't. But he embraced the priest.

And then he descended the narrow, winding stone staircase, his brother's figure disappearing above him.

Outside, the engine of the small green Fiat was purring. And behind the wheel, with the radio playing, was Sophia.

THE END

Fantastic Books
Great Authors

CROOKED
CAT

Meet our authors and discover
our exciting range:

- Gripping Thrillers
- Cosy Mysteries
- Romantic Chick-Lit
- Fascinating Historicals
- Exciting Fantasy
- Young Adult and Children's Adventures

Visit us at:
www.crookedcatbooks.com

Join us on facebook:
www.facebook.com/realcrookedcat

Made in the USA
Columbia, SC
16 October 2017